A Rush of Dreamers

A RUSH OF DREAMERS

★ ★ ★

BEING THE REMARKABLE STORY OF
NORTON I,
EMPEROR OF THE UNITED STATES
AND PROTECTOR OF MEXICO

John Cech

Marlowe
New York

Published by
Marlowe & Company
632 Broadway, Seventh Floor
New York, NY 10012

Copyright © 1997 by John Cech

All rights reserved. No part of this book may be reproduced in any form without written permission from the publishers, unless by reviewers who wish to quote brief passages.

Library of Congress Cataloging in Publication Data

Cech, John.
    A rush of dreamers, being the remarkable story of Joshua Norton : emperor of the united states and protector of mexico / by John Cech.
        p.   cm.
        ISBN 1-56924-775-7
        1. Norton, Joshua Abraham, 1819–1880—Fiction.
2. Eccentrics and eccentricities—California—San Francisco—Fiction. 3. Jews—California—San Francisco—Fiction. I. Title.
PS3553.E296R46   1997
813'.54—dc21   97-30231
                                                                                          CIP

Designed by Kathleen Lake

Manufactured in the United States of America.
First Edition

For John Weber and Charles DeFanti,
with deepest thanks for opening the door
to this dreamtime

Acknowledgments

A number of resources have proven to be invaluable in the research for this book. In particular, I wish to thank the Bancroft Library of the University of California at Berkeley for the use of their materials pertaining to the Emperor Norton and early California history; the San Francisco Public Library for their help in locating information about Addie L. Ballou; and Emily Wolf of the California Historical Society for her assistance with materials related to early photographic depictions of San Francisco, and, in particular, the Eadweard Muybridge panoramas of the city.

Of the books and many articles about Joshua Norton's life, I am most indebted to William Drury and his fine biography, *Norton I, Emperor of the United States*, which brings a thoroughness and joy to its subject and the historical background of the period that is truly remarkable and indispensible.

Marion Byrne and Wendy Moorehouse kept me posted concerning Norton's current presence in the Bay Area; Leah Karnatski cheerfully handled my seemingly endless calls and inquiries; and Daniel O'Connor calmly kept the project on track, despite all of the new, unexpected stations it needed to pass through. To all of you, I am most grateful.

Mara Lurie brought vital questions and a sense of perfect pitch to the final editing of the book; to her I send a very special note of thanks.

Beth Escott and JT Steiny have given the cover design its magic under circumstances that redefine the meaning of grace under pressure.

Alicia Nitecki's timely encouragement was essential to the launching of this journey. I'm glad she found the nugget that I hoped would be discovered in the book.

And, finally, always, my deep and loving thanks go to my daughter, Koren, and my wife, Eve, for listening to this story on its first, wobbly time through, for hearing it again and again until it found its legs, for giving it the best reception it could ever have had.

I

You wouldn't know my name. I'm not one of those famous fellows who have had their histories written down, those golden sons of California who came west in '49 with their noble deeds. But I was there and stood next to them at the bar. Most were decent enough and remained that way. Some were twisted by the place, and some were natural-born louts and swindlers. But the Emperor, he was different. I saw him when he first came off the *Franzeska* in the harbor and I saw him when he fell that last time in the rain on California Street. I know where he went in '59, after he lost everything, because I went too, and I know why he came back like he did and crowned himself Norton the First.

My friend Sam Clemens said I should tell the story.

"Write him up," he said in the Bank Exchange, and swallowed a whiskey punch on top of a hard-boiled egg. "You can't concoct a tale like that. It'll tell itself."

Sam tried to put the Emperor into that book he wrote about the boy named Huckleberry, called him a Dolphin, and made him into a slobbering windbag. And somewhere else he called him a beggar. The Emperor wouldn't have cared for that. He was a kind and serious man and not one for mockery. And surely not a moocher. He lived by his wits, but he wasn't a sponge. Not like some I could name but will not, some that rose to powerful places in this town, with their hands in everyone else's pie.

So I will tell the story of the Emperor, who was my friend, before somebody gets it wrong again.

★ ★ ★

Before I ever touched the Emperor's sleeve, I was just a printer's man in South Lancaster, smearing ink on Mr. Chandler's type, running his presses, twirling his rounces, nipping up with the best. When I wasn't keeping my fingers out of the frisket, I tried my hand at writing some. Maybe you've heard of *The Remarkable Story of Chicken Little*? I was twelve when I scratched that out one night and printed it for the holiday in 1840 when they set the memorial stone at Bunker Hill. It was my tale. Well, truth be told, it was my gram's. That little chicken's been in my family for years, but Mr. Chandler put it in his own pot. I was an apprentice then, and couldn't say a word about it. Who would have believed me anyway, me a printer's devil.

My great uncle Martin Hosmer secured me the aprenticeship with Chandler. Uncle Martin was a chapman, tromping the roads between Worcester and Lancaster, Putnam and Petersham. From his wagon he sold buttons and bows, combs and soap, shiny tin pots, and potions to cure any disorder, spools of thread, wooden nutmegs, candles, bowls and cloth, primers and bibles and, tucked away in the pockets of his greatcoat, copies of "Jack the Giant Killer" and "Little Red Cap," along with the puppets he made out of old stockings for the shows he did for the kiddies on the farms. Uncle Martin was inspired on one trip to give Chicken Little his first run around the barnyard. He told me he made up Loosey Goosey's name and a lot of the other daffy stuff in the story to pull a chuckle out of those tight Yankee parents, and maybe get them to take a knot or two out of their purse strings.

A little while after that Uncle Martin was tromping over George Hill Road, stopped to water his horse at Chandler's place, and heard that he needed a boy to lock the quoins. He told him he knew of a good lad and wrote my folks in Hancock. So down I came with our neighbor William Elliot, taking oxen to Worcester in the spring of 1838. I was ten.

When Chandler moved to Boston to build that grand house on Boylston Street, I stayed behind with ink on my hands and a bitterness in my heart in those drafty rooms above the shop, trying to rhyme out my future. The sky wasn't falling, but I wasn't going anyplace either.

I wasn't old, but neither was I a boy. Twenty when the papers from Boston arrived that Friday in December. President Polk announced to the nation what everyone knew already—there was gold at Sutter's Mill in California. The news took fire in our commonwealth like a spark in a hayrick. Everybody buzzed around it, especially after the papers printed letters about how they were finding more gold in a week than a good mechanic made in a year, or a saved in a lifetime. I kept the articles. Kept them all the way to California. And I used them to wipe my arse, eventually.

But that was later.

★ ★ ★

I was on the post coach that returned to Boston on Saturday, bouncing over those infernal ruts through Stow and down to Concord, and sloshing into Cambridge and then to the Charles, over the bridge and slowly on, for it was snowing hard, sliding over the icy cobbles to the Common.

I had six hundred dollars in a pouch tied to my belt, double-knotted tight and tucked inside the top of my trousers. Five hundred of that was my legacy that my brother, Benjamin, brought to me in my last year at Chandler's. It was half of what he got for the farm. My fair share, he said. Ben was two years older than me, solitary, frugal in his speech. But he was not selfish, and there was true brotherly affection between us. Without complaint, he added my work to his after I left to be apprenticed. All was well until Mother died of consumption, and the next spring Father fell from the barn rafters loading in the June cutting. May they be at peace. So the farm was sold, and Ben delivered my portion on his way to Hartford to find his luck. He wished me Godspeed, kicked the side of our big plow horse, Rocker, and they plodded on down the pike.

Not like the Ford brothers in Hollis. The two of them were ever quarreling, and that was why their father, Zerrubbabel, buried his gold in the woods behind the house. With his will he left instructions that read: "Dear Sons, If you will take ten long paces East from the oak tree and four short paces South, dig down three feet and you shall have your inheritance." But he never said which oak to start *from*. There were over a hundred scattered on those acres that had never been logged off. He thought such a test would lead to fraternal cooperation and harmony. But the brothers fought and dug, dug and fought. In time they fell out altogether, each calling the other blinding names. They divided up the land, equally, and then they sawed the house in half. Tyler dragged his portion down the lane, out of sight of his brother, Lyman, who lived in the other half. They did not pass another word to each other in this world. They dug in that yard all their lives, on alternating days so they would not have to meet. They never did. And they never found the gold.

★ ★ ★

The docks were crowded with men like me, and some women too, looking for boats to take them round the Horn. The clippers were a rich man's ride—one thousand dollars for the passage. So I kept looking. I found a boat soon enough—a bark called the *Coventry*, out of Marblehead. She was freshly painted to hide the rot, but she had new canvas and was ready to sail for the goldfields once the captain, a Connecticut man with watery blue eyes named Orson Palmer, could finish loading for the passage round the Cape. Five months of that if we were lucky. Maybe you got the clap in Rio, but it wouldn't be cholera in Chagres—the way across the isthmus to Panama and the Pacific.

Captain Palmer knocked the snow off the brim of his hat and looked me over not unkindly and inquired, "Can you cook, son?"

Seems their cook had fallen asleep drunk in the courtyard behind North Church and never woke up again.

"If you can fashion something savory from those barrels of hardtack," he went on, pointing to the hogsheads that were even then being lowered into the dark hold of the *Coventry*, "you'll be worth your weight in gold. You can go half price—two hundred and fifty."

"I think I can do as much," I told him cheerfully, hoping that he thought I meant the price more than my duties.

But I truly thought I could pull off the cooking, having watched my gram hover over the hearth for years after I had done my lessons, listening to her steady patter of words. I had even printed a book for Chandler concerning Escoffier's gastronomical delights for the Emperor Napoleon's table. I hoped I could discover the ingredients for a marsala in the galley, even if I had to use a rat instead of chicken.

"You had better be as good as your word, my boy," he said tersely, "or the crew will be carving you for dinner."

★ ★ ★

The *Coventry* was under a commission from groups of fortune seekers who occupied the cabins and the other best spots aboard. Most of the boats in the harbor were. All were headed for the new strikes on the American River above Sutter's Mill. These enterprising travelers had capital behind them, to stake them in their ventures. To family and friends and neighbors they promised shares of the profits they would reap in that glorious land where gold was as ordinary as pebbles in a stream. Had not those same letters in the papers all said that you could gather gold up from the ground, or scoop it with a soup spoon from the side of a stream? We would arrive in late springtime, if we were lucky. The end of summer would see us all sailing home rich men, back to the arms of our loved ones. I must say they were giddy with the thought of it. We all were.

There was a group aboard that called itself the Harvard Company, a dozen young men from the college who had thrown their fortunes together. The father of one gave a speech as we were making ready to sail. "Go forth," he orated. "Go forth and pluck the riches from that wild land on our continent's farthest shore. Go forth, with God's blessing to guide you, with his angels on your shoulders. But do not forget your loved ones in the land of the heathens, the Spanish Papists, and the red savages. Do not forget your dear homes, where lights will be kept burning in your memory. Do not forget, you precious sons of New England, to remember your heritage, to live with honor and find your way back to us. Go forth, you Argonauts on your great journey, and return to us, heroes, triumphant from the quest with your golden fleece."

We would be fleeced, right enough, but no one knew that then.

II

But of course you wanted to know about the Emperor.

Everyone has his favorite stories about the man, and they bring them out at banquets and parties, when liquor has filled them with good cheer, and they want to touch that strange greatness again that used to walk our streets.

Like I said, I remember him when he was fresh off the boat, when he set his first foot down on these shores.

I was there on the wharf when his ship, the German boat *Franzeska*, landed on November twenty-third. I was passing out leaflets to the passengers, telling them of Mrs. Palmer's boardinghouse, the Birches, offering to walk them there in the fading afternoon light, holding a lantern next to the most amiable face I could make, leaning on my stick to keep weight off my leg.

And here comes the Emperor. He was first in line to climb off the boat. He wasn't the Emperor then to be sure, just Joshua Norton, from Algoa Bay at the tip of Africa, thirty-one years old, an Englishman, a Jew, and a man itching to get ahead, like all others, Hebrew, gentile, or oriental, who had braved the sea or land to reach this place. He had brought forty thousand dollars with him to start himself off, I later learned, all that was left to him by his father, poor man, who died in England trying to find a rabbi to bring God's ancient word back to Africa. Not long after that Norton lost his mother as well, and his two brothers, Louis and Philip, in the few years before he came. There was nothing to keep him there. No sweetheart, no friends. Only sad memories which he'd rather leave.

Norton was impatient to be off that wharf, to find a proper place to stay, to get started. Already he thought of himself as a businessman of some stature, though he was a small man, about five and a half feet tall, a little portly from the lassitude of the sea voyage, and going bald on top.

"It's not far, and after your voyage, the walk will do you good," I told him when he inquired after the lodgings I offered. "Here, let me help you with your bags."

"Indeed not, sir," he said in a clipped English accent, and held tightly to the suitcase and carpet bag he had carried down the planks from the ship.

"Mind your step," I told him, leading him by the elbow through the jostling maze of people and cargo on the pier.

"Sir," he insisted, his mutton chop whiskers and thick mustaches bristling, "I can comport myself without your help."

He balanced his valises in either hand, and together we trudged up Broad Street, picking our way between the wagon ruts and the debris that lay upon the ground or was half-submerged in the mud—whiskey bottles and oyster tins, the remains of rats and, every few yards, an odiforous manure pile—road nuggets, we called them, free for the taking. Already there had been heavy rain, and the roads were criss-crossed with ruts that had filled with water. Large puddles blocked progress on every block and had to be carefully circumnavigated.

But Norton proceeded straight ahead, oblivious to the dangers beneath his feet, tramping over protruding obstacles as though they were mere twigs on a country lane, and he out for a stroll.

"Mind your step," I warned him, again reaching for his arm to guide him around the edge of a packing crate jutting up from the roadway like an angry plough blade bent on furrowing someone's shin.

But he angrily shrugged my hand away again. "Really, sir, there's no need for you to guide me like some blind old fool. I can fend for myself. Please allow me to do so or I shall find some other accommodations.

"Suit yourself," I said. "But for heaven's sake mind how you go. You know, just the other day, a mule . . . "

I had led Norton around a corner, swinging in a wide arc with my lantern to avoid a large puddle. It was the turn for Happy Valley and Mrs. Palmer's. I fully expected Norton to follow me, yet he had continued straight ahead.

". . . stepped into the puddle we just passed and disappeared without a trace."

"Oh, dear!" I heard him cry above the noise of the traffic in the road.

I thought at last that I had impressed caution upon him and turned to look at my irascible but now enlightened companion only to discover he had disappeared.

I raced to the edge of the puddle and saw bubbles on the surface of the water. Reaching down into that black wallow, I somehow secured his coat collar, and with it hauled him out onto the muddy road. He coughed and spat the filthy water from his mouth, but he was still clutching his valises. How I lifted that weight, I shall never know.

So you might say that I was there when the Emperor made his first big splash in San Francisco. And you might say that I rescued one of its favorite sons from an ignoble demise on his arrival in town.

He caught his breath, choked and sputtered, spat and retched, poor man. I thumped on his back and dabbed a kerchief over his face despite his curses.

"What a hell hole!" he cried. "This is a place of offal and filth. Why did you not properly warn me? You have brought me here to drown me like a rat in that puddle and abscond with my belongings."

"Now, now," I said. "I pulled you out of that muck, didn't I? Why would I go to the trouble of saving you if I just wanted your shirts and socks? Now why don't I just leave you here, and we'll see who'll take you in."

"Indeed, you will not," he shot back at me. "You promised me fair and honest lodgings, and you are bound by your word to provide them."

"But you've just accused me of being an assassin," I replied. "It would serve you well."

Norton payed little attention to my words. The full force of the odor he was emitting had finally overwhelmed his nostrils.

"What is that smell?" Norton twisted his nose with disgust.

"Shit, mostly," I said. "Maybe some dead mule as well. But it belongs to you now. Welcome to San Francisco."

This time I took him firmly by the arm and escorted him without protest the half mile to Mrs. Palmer's, where he was greeted with a bath, a bowl of hot stew, and a good night's rest in the royal suite: a cot in the very last cubicle of her lodgers' tent, with ivy painted on the canvas, entwining the trunks of the painted birches.

While the Emperor sleeps his first sleep in the city, I should tell you the rest of my story, and Mrs. Palmer's too.

III

It was a long trip 'round, me swinging in my hammock between the carving board and the stove, the other gold hunters heaving over the side. We froze all the way through January, tacking across the Atlantic and nearly to dark Africa. It took us twenty days to reach those God-forsaken islands of Cape Verde that climb out of the sea and are not green at all. Then we set a new course, south by southwest, to take us down to Rio. All the while, I served up stew and watery soup with that dry Boston bread. No one minded, those that could keep anything down, so long as it was hot.

They had even given me a helper, a German named Eric Vetter, a tall, raw-boned boy with a gap-toothed grin and nails he had bitten to the quick. He had been a drummer boy in the Prussian army but ran away because of the beatings they gave him. He broke the skins and flubbed the sticks because he couldn't seem to get used to the idea of being in the vanguard of a company that was marching into the teeth of a fusillade. So he slipped away one night, stole clothes hanging out to dry in a farmer's yard, and hoofed it to Lübeck, where he stowed away on a ship bound for Boston with porcelain and church glass. They caught him and beat him, which he took as his fare, for they were well at sea, and put him to work. They turned him over to the constabulary when the ship arrived in port. Six months in Boston Lock-up, where he was scourged by his Irish guards and taught enough of the President's English to plead for mercy. When they tired of whipping him, they set him free. He lived in barrels and packing cases along the quays, until Palmer saw him one cold morning in December and hired him as a ship's boy.

The first mate of the *Coventry* would lash him with a length of rope if he didn't move quickly enough on his deck duties. And he gave Eric some of the dirtiest work—emptying and swabbing the latrine buckets. But Eric did not complain, even though his fingers were red and raw from lye.

"My parents did not luf me," he told me one day, when he was peeling the last of the potatoes. "Zay ver so poor, zay sold me to zee armay. Sum day I vill be rich and go back, and zen zay vill luf me."

We crossed the Line and performed those peculiar rites that sailors visit on their passengers and any new members of the crew who have not passed this way before. They pulled me from the galley to receive my proper baptism from King Poseidon. They said it was

Madeira, but it smelled like a pisspot to me, which they followed with buckets of cold saltwater down my neck to complete my ordeal. I thought to myself, "I could tinkle in your porridge, messmates, and you'll never know it. Then who will have the last laugh?"

I should have, too, but I did not twitch for revenge. However, I did leave the chowder uncovered some days later when I brought the pot out to serve the crew. A sea bird shat in it. Quite by accident. No, I did not wish it. Yet I did not tell a soul, just mixed it into the broth and stuck with hardtack that day.

"Good chowder," growled the first mate. "About time you put some flavor innit." The mate was one Lemuel Nast, a small man with a bulbous nose and bulging eyes, who drove the newer men like slaves and let his chums nap in the lifeboats. He watched me from my first morning on board, and counted every bag, every speck of meat and drop of suet. He made sure he and his cronies got the biggest helpings. He woke me in the morning with a kick against my leg—until I began to rise before him.

"He puts quite a snout in the trough," one of the foretop men, Andrew Godwin, said to me over his plate of grub.

I thought about that and asked Mr. Nast if he'd like a bit more.

"A course," he grunted, gobbling his soup. "'Bout time you asked."

I made sure to get my ladle into a little pool of something with green flecks floating on it to add to his bowl.

My duties were simple: Keep the kettles simmering with tea and coffee—all day and all night. Mind the fire so that it doesn't leap out of the stove when the ship stands on end. Make pots of chowder or stew with any ingredients at hand—salted meat, fish, and even a sea bird or two if I could snare the stringy things. Bake bread every third day, deter the rats with my cleaver if they escaped our traps, and boil the maggots in the meat until they both looked alike.

Captain Palmer was smart. He brought along baskets of limes and lemons to keep away the scurvy. And he stocked up with bags of rice, which kept longer and better than flour. He'd been around the Horn on the China run, and he knew his ropes. He put up with Nast because the runt got the job done and could sniff out trouble among the men or changes in the weather with that big nose of his. Maybe Captain Palmer knew himself to be too easy and he understood he must have a Nast. Maybe he thought the Dwarf, for that is what all called him outside his hearing, made him look even better than he was. Perhaps it made him feel content to be the good master while Nast squeaked and squalled at the men and oozed over the important passengers.

Palmer brought his wife along on the trip. Charlotte. A hearty soul, she wanted to see the gold country and not another lonely Cape Anne winter. She was born and bred in Boston, could quote the Bard freely, and had a ready, cheerful laugh. She also had a most generous heart, and her natural compassion led her to take pity on me.

She arrived at my galley early the morning after she had sampled my errant cornbread that crumbled in everyone's hands before they could get it to their lips. She showed me how to fold in enough lard to hold the thing together, which I did for days, until the lard turned putrid, and after that I followed her recipe and mixed the meal into the morning porridge. She often cheered me up with her visits during the long tedium of the voyage, and she never criticized even my most pathetic dish. When I asked her how she liked it, she would simply emit a noncommittal *"Aaaaaaaa"*— which spoke volumes about my bouillabaisse.

★ ★ ★

Along with the Harvards, that I've spoken of, there were two other groups of about a dozen or more members each that had hired the *Coventry* in the first place—the Ipswich Enterprise and the Lexington Consortium. Like the others, they had sold shares in their endeavor, bought equipment, and agreed to work together and divide their fortunes equally. These were serious men, young and old alike, who might have been lawyers or physicians had they not decided to search for gold. But aboard our ship they were all bankers. They talked business stratagems, percentages and capital investments, markets and mortgages. They debated, discussed, wrote, and ratified articles of incorporation for their groups with various commandments to honor the flag and Christian virtue, the fair sex and the holiness of the sabbath, to eschew swearing or the imbibing of strong liquors. They promised their sweethearts that they would not succumb to the frailties of the flesh. What fun was to be left them in this world, I can not begin to fathom.

Outside the groups, the rest of the passengers were a muddled lot—thirty-three in all when we began—stacked everywhere in the holds and even some encamped on deck. There were several boys from Groton, the Ginn brothers, fifteen and seventeen, cheerful pudgy lads with a guitar and a fife, who regaled us with drinking songs for the first hour we were sailing till they began to heave the remnants of their last Boston meal into their instruments.

A preacher and his wife, Amos and Elizabeth Winchell, off to bring God's word to the diggings, led us in Sunday services. We had among us a carpenter (Theodore Hightalling), a stonemason (Michael Larsen), several drovers, a handful of mechanics, a farmer or two, a viniculturalist from France, a surgeon, a chap who had sold his orchards in Acton to finance his venture, several lumbermen from Casco, two clerks from Boston barristers, and a dozen others whose names and occupations I forget. I remember something about many of their faces, though. They glowed as though some inner light was radiating outward from within. Their eyes in particular held a fire, a spark of something I cannot name in this world, something fierce, unquenchable, and strangely beautiful.

JOHN CECH

★ ★ ★

By February we were able to see the coast of Brazil. The days were warm, and at night we lay out on the deck and told our dreams and debated the nature of this life. A soft-spoken schoolmaster from Arlington, Mr. Brantley, often led the evenings with a topic for the general edification of the ship.

"Resolved," he would say, and wait for the attention of those on deck before he went on. "Resolved that, by the Grace of God, mankind is nearing the pinnacle of its perfection and that we can only expect an ever more harmonious state for humanity in the future."

And the debate would begin, seesawing for the rest of the evening with the rolling of the ship.

"If things are so perfect," offered a sharp-tongued fellow from Framingham, who cared little for the sea, the glow of whose face was in complete eclipse, "what are we doing on this leaking tub?"

"Aye," added another who was having second thoughts. "Why must we leave our homes and families to scratch while we risk everything in some valley on the other side of the world. If things were perfect, we'd be sitting close to our own, making a decent living."

"Ah," Brantley went on, "but even this adventure is part of the perfection—to be in search, not for some substance that will merely sustain a mean and petty existence—a sack of potatoes, perhaps, or a basket of turnips or apples—but for gold, the most noble of minerals, the goal of ancient philosophers and kings."

"Perhaps, sir, you are mistaking necessity for nobility," replied his challenger. "You can't even have a mean and petty existence without a little gold to buy your potatoes, now can you?"

It took another month to reach that still and majestic harbor, and along the way we argued about Mr. Emerson's Transcendentalism and whether or not God might appear to us as a transparent eyeball in the woods ("Only if you're drinking varnish," said Hightalling the carpenter), Original Sin ("Only if it was originally summun else's," the drover from Bellerica quipped), and the ability of spirits to communicate to the world of the living by means of rappings heard emanating from the houses they inhabited.

"I'll converse with any spirit that comes tapping about my house with a rap of a belaying pin," snarled Nast on that occasion.

Brantley suspended the debating society after this, and we all settled, if the sea was quiet, to songs and stories. I read to them from the books I had brought with me from Chandler's and told the story of the Ford brothers in Hollis, the divided house, their fighting and digging in the woods, and the unfound gold.

"A worthy parable," said Preacher Winchell. "It instructs us not to forget the true nature of brotherhood."

"Why do you tell such a sad story about brothers?" asked Rupert Ginn. "Thomas and I would never fight so over a few pieces of gold."

"Nor would we," said one of the Harvard fellows, who was also traveling with his brother.

"You'll squabble with your brother soon enough," Nast interjected, "when it comes to a fistful of gold."

And so went the debate until Thomas Ginn ended it with the chords of "Oh, Susanna," and we all sang it through to the end:

> *I soon shall be in Frisco,*
> *And there I'll look around,*
> *And when I see the Gold lumps there*
> *I'll pick them off the ground.*
> *I'll scrape the mountains clean, my boys,*
> *I'll drain the rivers dry,*
> *A pocketful of rocks bring home—*
> *So brothers don't you cry!*
> *Oh, California,*
> *That's the land for me!*
> *I'm bound for San Francisco*
> *With my washbowl on my knee.*

★ ★ ★

Because the work was so light and routine, the crew was quickly bored, Nast in particular. He used his extra time to torment Eric, even though the boy was taller than he and much stronger. He began to wake him for his watch by pulling on the hairs of his legs which dangled over the edge of his bunk. And he took to ridiculing the boy's speech.

"Ach, Eric," he would say, "gif us a kiss on die assenheimer."

Eric would be held to the spot, speechless, by the taunting.

One day Nast tripped the lad as he was carrying the slop bucket from the kitchen. Its contents puddled across the common-room floor, and Eric, facedown, slid upon its surface.

"Vatch dein steppen, du oaf," Nast lashed out at him. "Quick. Look lively, shitfurfeet. Clean it up. Or veel be trowing use over de side mit de slops."

"Leave him alone," I ordered Nast, who had his back to me while he continued to enjoy Eric's mortification.

"And who might that be?" he asked as he turned. "Mercy, it's the cook."

"I said to leave him. This is my galley."

"Trouble is, it's on my ship."

"I'm warning you, Nast," I said, taking a step toward him.

Nast's bulging eyes had noticed the large knives that I held in both hands.

"You'd better watch your step, cook. Mind that you don't fall into the hole that you've just dug for yourself. It's a deep and a dark one," he said as he backed out of the common room.

From that day on, I had to guard the galley. If I left it for any length of time, soup would be spoiled, the fire extinguished, a turd left in the oven.

★ ★ ★

In Rio we took on supplies and patched up the

Coventry, especially along the keel that had opened up in the rough seas at midocean. I helped to load strange fruits by the basketful, with more salted pork and biscuits as dry as an August afternoon.

A peddler on the dock offered me something.

"Bing lock," he said, and showed me a necklace made from bones and yellow feathers. "Zis make shou rich," he tugged on my sleeve. "Uno dollar."

I did not crave this token, but I gave him the dollar in coins from the sack around my neck. He smiled and tied the necklace there, too.

"Leef shere," he commanded, smiling a grin of black teeth, and disappeared into the crowd.

★ ★ ★

The days were long in those tropical waters. Everyone spent as much time as they could on deck because below was close and rank with farts and sweat and tar and bilge. Some wrote their journals, others dozed in the sun, and the discussions now turned to what the argonauts would do with their riches.

"It is only right that some be shared with the poor and less fortunate," maintained Parson Winchell.

"Let the poor dig for themselves," replied one Ronald Jones, whose father was a banker and helped finance the Ipswich company. "They're not our responsibility."

"But you are your brother's keeper, are you not?" asked the Parson.

"Not in the least. This is the United States of America, not some infernal principality. We're free men here. Free to work and prosper. And if one doesn't," Jones concluded with a flourish, "well, it's his own damned fault."

The conversation drifted up through the rigging. Martin Sampson, a Freemason who was headed for the goldfields with several others of that fraternity spoke up. "We believe that all men are brothers."

"They ain't all my brothers," Hightalling the carpenter added.

"Man's proper state is more like swine," opined our first mate, who was passing by and now joined in. "Much as your fine talk would like to make it otherwise, can anybody really argue with the motto: 'Root, hog, or die?'"

"You should be ashamed of yourself to propose such a thing," said Parson Winchell. "Don't you know the difference between true self-interest and venal greed?"

"I know the difference," Nast replied, "between having my belly and pockets full and being robbed by every sluggard who happens to want what's in mine." With that he sent a long, precise gob of spit arching over the railing and into the sea.

★ ★ ★

All arguments and disquisitions stopped when we reached the Cape.

Our ship stood on its nose and then on its arse in the pitching waves. I thought the waves would tear the planks loose and sweep us all out of our bunks and into that cold sea. We were wet for three weeks, fighting the wind and the currents down halfway to that land of ice, then up north again, and inch by inch slowly west.

Nast screamed at the men over the gales that aroused themselves, one after the other, to pommel the sides of the *Coventry*. I doled out hardtack and biscuits on the wildest days, since I didn't dare a fire, and managed to add tea on the others when the pitching subsided.

I won't tell you about the vomit that ran across the deck when all the passengers became sick again, or the numbers who soiled their own trousers when a wave rose to the height of our mainmast, or of the man whose heart froze in the night from fear. No, I should not tell you of any of these things. Most adventures are composed of puke and piss and perseverance. Who would go on any if they knew this before they left?

Captain Palmer barely quit the deck, except to steal a few hours sleep. He wore only a light oilskin coat, even though he was soaked to the bone. His wife came on deck with sweets and other things she had packed away for him, and glasses of tea that she managed to brew in their cabin, laced with honey and rum and cloves. If he was cold, he never said so, though his hands shook when he took the cup.

Other vessels were tossed on those waves with us. For most of a day we heaved near one of the great clippers out of New York, the *Davy Crockett*, its long, sleek hull showing up our stubby, shabby shape. Like us, she was trying to hold a course and tack in one of those fierce gales. Even her lights and tall masts disappeared behind the height of the waves. She had overtaken us, hailed us, her captain shouting greetings through his horn, and once she could make some westerly headway, she left us to flounder on by ourselves.

Twenty-three days of this.

Until we finally broke free and sailed into the Pacific on April twelfth. Within a day the winds had dropped and we could make an easy run up to Valparaiso for fresh provisions and to rest our aching bodies.

★ ★ ★

The Chilianos are a hard people. Sour and unfriendly. At least those in that city were. They lock up their daughters, of course—who would not with a pack of hot young men like us around. A few of our party had letters of introduction to the Governor and businessmen in the city, and they were treated well, like visiting notables and long-awaited cousins. But the rest of us had to make do with tortillas, beans, cold shoulder, and the curfew that kept us off the streets after nine o'clock.

Valparaiso isn't much of a town. Adobe buildings with earthen floors. Some fancier homes for the quality. A plaza with scrubby trees ringing it, where the Governor marched his soldiers around three times a day.

The only thing I wanted was a walk on solid land and a glass of milk. The walk was better than the milk.

Many Chilianos had already left for the goldfields up north. A priest spit when we passed by and railed at us, part in his tongue, part in ours:

"May you choke on your gold. May your bowels be plugged up with it. May you never again have a pleasing shit in your lifetime. May your wife be a whore and your children steal your last peso before they wipe their asses on your memory. Curse all of you for taking our sons away, for making our wives widows, for turning our girls into sluts."

"He blames us for that?" I asked Captain Palmer, after he translated for me the words that I did not understand.

"Yep."

★ ★ ★

We followed the coast for several weeks. Then Captain Palmer began tacking northwest, and we lost sight of those blue shapes on the horizon. We had calm weather. My kitchen returned to normal. I even contrived to serve a good meal of seabird stew with some sourdough bread baked from Chiliano flour, with tomatoes, and some new beer from the casks we'd taken on in Valparaiso.

I asked Captain Palmer about our course and why we were sailing into the sun in the afternoon.

"We've got to swing out west to get a run at the Golden Gate," he replied.

"What is that?"

"It's what the entrance to the harbor is called. It's a tight fit." He winked. "Like a Beacon Hill virgin. So we tack n'west halfway to the Sandwiches if we have to, just a whisker under thirty-eighth parallel, and then catch the west winds for San Francisco and hope we don't miss the opening and end up on the rocks."

We turned east on May twenty-ninth, my dear mother's birthday, and rode a steady wind through those peaks that guard the opening to that lovely harbor. Captain Palmer's touch on the wheel was peerless.

We glided past several islands in the bay that were covered with small, twisted pines and other trees I didn't know, and past the small fort on the right.

"This place used to be called 'Yerba Buena,'" Rupert Ginn said. He read from one of the guide books that was tucked into half the traveler's packs on board and whose usefulness ended with such illuminations. "That means the place of 'Good Herbs.'"

The *Coventry* rounded the sand spit and we stood at the rail in amazement. Nearly four hundred vessels, of every rig and nation, were swinging at anchor in the harbor. The whole was bathed in gold and purple evening light. Dozens of haphazard buildings and tents ran up the sandy hills from the shore. We had thought, of course, that we would be the first, and someone said as much.

"Had you expected a band to be playing on the dock? Had you expected your fathers to be here to welcome you?" Nast added sourly.

We anchored near a French cutter and a brig from Savannah, both dark, their ropes swinging on the waves and the faint sounds of metal on wood playing over the water like a sprung pianoforte. A few scattered lanterns burned on several of the ships, but otherwise all was black and still on the water, while on the shore many small flickering lights climbed up the hills and dunes in the coming darkness.

It was too late to go ashore, to find our way among these hulking wooden islands. We spent a restless night in speculation, eager to be off.

It wasn't until the next morning, when the harbormaster's boat rowed out to meet us, that we discovered the reason for the quiet on all these ships.

"They've all gone to the diggins," the rheumatic officer announced. "Near every last one of 'em."

We questioned him about the best way to get to the goldfields.

"Well, you can walk," he said, scratching his purple nose. "That'll take you a week or two, if you don't mind the bears. But it's free."

"Or you can ride," he went on, "if you have a horse, which I plainly see you don't. Or you can take the steamer up to Sacramento. Cost you ten dollars if you're lucky enough to get a seat. You'll be there this evening, or tomorrow morning if it's slow."

We spent the rest of the day unloading the *Coventry* and her passengers, making trip after trip through the maze of boats to bring everyone ashore, where they disappeared like raindrops in the sand. I saw the Ginn brothers go rolling up the rutted path that led from the beach, loaded down with their packs and suitcases. The

Harvard fellows had piled their gear onto the barrows they had brought with them and pushed these up the hill. The parson and his wife headed for a tent with a cross on it—their black clothes already spattered with mud.

Close to the shore, just a few hundred feet beyond the high-tide line, sat a low building with a sign that read CITY HOTEL on its roof. A veranda ran around three sides. Most of the passengers ended up there first, and found out that they would have to pay twenty-five dollars a night for a room, if there was one; five dollars for a bunk in a room with thirty or forty others, if a place could be found among the fleas. Most trudged up the hills to the shacks and tents marked HOTEL, with boards painted onto their canvas sides, and paid a few dollars for some shelter from the cool misty wind that was moving in from the ocean.

I stayed on the *Coventry* with the Palmers and the crew, listening to the lonely sounds of those empty ships another night. Captain Palmer had finally gone to bed, exhausted. Come morning, the Palmers and I had our own boat to ourselves. All the crew had deserted. Palmer had only paid them half their wages, the rest was due them back in Boston, but still they left. Even Nast. They pilfered the ship's arms, the lifeboats, and any goods they could carry. It took us till mid morning to hail a rowboat stopping at a nearby ship. He only spoke French, but we told him with gestures what we wanted.

"Teen books!" he yelled across the water, holding up as many fingers. We offered him five, but he shook his head. We settled on seven and paid our toll and took our sodden ride to shore.

Palmer managed to locate a boat from the *Coventry* among the dozens abandoned in the muck.

"We'll stay on the boat, Mrs. Palmer and me," he said. "It'll be safer there. We'll be along as soon as we get our stores ashore and the ship secured."

He gave me a clap on the back and shook my hand.

"Good luck to you, laddie," he said, his blue eyes swimming. "If you see Nast, tell him he owes me seven dollars, and then some. You can collect it from him."

Eric and I tramped up the hill, through the muddy sand, with what gear we had and the food the Palmers had given us, in sacks over our shoulders. Eric had decided to attach his destiny to mine and followed without hesitation. The porch outside the hotel was crowded with miners in their torn, dirty clothing and new arrivals like us, in our own threadbare duds. I struck up a conversation with an old fellow dressed in buckskin, sitting in the shade of the porch, and asked him about getting to the diggings.

"The boat ain't back yet," he said. "You'll know when it is by the sound of it. Be sure to get down there fast if you want a seat."

"What about a kit? Tools?"

"All you needs 's a shovel, a pick, and a pan."

"Where'll I find those?"

"Well, you can have mine," he replied, pointing to his gear against the wall. "For fifty dollars."

"Won't you be needing them?"

"Naw, I've been to see the elephant."

"An elephant?"

"The diggins, boy. Took every last penny we had, left my wife alone on the farm, and came down here from the Willamette up in Oregon country. I curse the day I ever left. Worked for a year on the placers up above Sutter's Mill, where the first was found. Worked all the way up the American River, all the way to Dutch Flats, and you know what I got in return for a year of freezin' and shiverin' in those streams? Know what I got for diggin' from dawn till dark? Know what I got for fighting off bears and snakes and claim jumpers? For a year of that I got me seventy-five dollars and some change. Let me give you a piece of advice, son. Stay here and be a carpenter or a tailor or a cook. Be anything your heart wants to be. But don't be a miner. Let the gold come to you a different way. Let some other poor fuddle like me dig it out."

"We'll find something. I know it," I responded.

"You'll find something, all right. Piles of woe and sacks of misery is what you'll get if'n you're lucky. But I can see you've made your mind up. At least you're young—and you've got your partner there," he pointed at Eric, who hung on every word.

"Where should we dig?"

"There's people most everywhere now," he said, wiping his hand across his eyes. "But you might try going up to them Russian digs on the North Fork of the American. Bi-lee-something. I don't know. But the name means 'White.' Russians are good people—they were here before us, trapping and trading with the Injuns. At least they'll share a piece of bread with you—not like most Yankees I know, or the scum that's come out from Missouri country, or them vipers from Sidney down under. They'll carve off your toes and fry 'em like sausages if you give 'em a chance. Yessir, try the Russian diggins on the North."

"But I don't know any Russian."

"Can you sing?"

"A bit."

"Well, just sing around the Russians and you'll be fine. They love a song and a drink."

"Here, you take this too," he said, handing me a small stone, jagged and milky white, with flecks of something yellow in the crystals.

"That there is quartz, with gold in it. Now you know what it looks like."

I paid him for his tools, though I knew it was too much, and for his advice, though I didn't think I'd need it. I walked up to the top of the hill straight ahead of me and turned and looked down at the harbor below and its hundreds of ghost ships riding high on the morning tide. The mist had burned off and the hills on the west side of the bay were golden in the morning sun. The hills that ringed the bay on the east were green in this light. Beyond them riches awaited us, wealth enough to draw people from halfway round the world to reach, and it was there for the taking. I pitied the poor miner at the hotel.

"We'll be lucky," I said to myself as much as to Eric. And I rubbed the yellow feathers on the charm around my neck. I hadn't thought about it much, but now I did.

We ate some biscuits from the *Coventry* and drank a bottle of wine left behind in the ship's stores and thought about what we might do with our first pounds of gold. The morning passed, bright and brisk, and I drifted off to sleep, against the pack.

The long blasts of a boat whistle roused me from a dream of rowing, rowing against a fast-moving current. I could see down the hill a white paddle steamer, making for a rough dock planted in the harbor. I nudged Eric and pointed to the boat. We hurried to pull our things together. I hitched the old man's pack onto my back, and we headed quickly down the hill.

The side-wheeler *Zeus* was unloading its passengers when we arrived, panting, to find ourselves thick in a throng of others, clamoring to get aboard. They'd appeared out of the dunes, we thought.

"Easy, folks, easy," one of the crew yelled. "Save your shoving for the diggings. The gold will wait till you get there."

"Yeah," someone leaving the boat spat, "and it'll still be there when you're wore out."

Slowly, it unloaded its passengers and then the stevedores wheeled aboard the goods that were waiting on the makeshift dock. Sacks of flour and beans, rice and baskets of vegetables, tenting and tools, and, most precious of all, kegs of spirits which were rolled onto the deck and lashed down.

Only then were the passengers let on. Perhaps a hundred people and their belongings, which set the boat low, just a few inches above the waterline. We couldn't get near the dock, let alone the boat. When the deckhands closed the entryway, a groan issued from the waiting crowd, followed by curses in many languages, hands raised in fists, a spent apple core or two hurled at the sailors.

"I've already been waiting three days," said the pudgy man next to me. He wore a black suit and a flat straw hat. He had strapped a leather suitcase on his back and carried two bags made out of old carpeting in each hand.

"Where have you stayed?" I asked him above the din.

"Over yonder," he gestured behind him with a throw of his head, back up the shore where I could see a small city of tenting sprawled along and among the low hills and dunes.

"There's hundreds waiting to find some way inland to the diggings. I don't know when I'll ever get aboard."

He led me to where he had camped and to the hollow he'd dug in the sandy earth to shield himself from the harbor winds.

"Name's Steven Lyons," he held out his hand.

I took it and shook it. We camped together in the valley with the other gold seekers and their tents and blankets, the smoke from their fires drifting in a blue haze over the camp and told our stories over beans.

Lyons came west from Chicago by steamer down the Mississippi to New Orleans and from there to Chagres, up the Chagres River and over the mountains to Panama City, and then up the coast by steamer to California. He was fortunate to have made it so quickly. Many got stuck in Panama for months.

"There's nothing for me in Chicago except a broken back. I laid brick for a dollar or two a day. Anyhows, if my boss or his boys ever find me again, they'll lay some bricks atop my head. Caught me lowing among the cows in the stable with his daughter. You can guess the rest."

It was rent-free. So we stayed. They called the place Happy Valley. The winds blew sand into everything, but at least it also carried away the stink of the toilets everyone had carved into the dunes.

I bought a bowl of stringy dough from a cauldron of soup in front of a Chinese tent. Noodles.

I watched Kanakas from the Sandwiches play a game with grunts and shouts and a handful of knuckle bones.

I listened to the songs the Chilianos played on their guitars.

A Frenchman wandered through the camp declaiming poetry, I think.

I visited with some of my old companions, from the *Coventry*, who were camped out as well: Hightalling and his friends, the lumbermen from Maine.

I think I heard the Ginn brothers playing over the next dune as I was drifting off to sleep.

I dreamed of an orchard full of ripe peaches.

Every time there was a stirring in the crowd, we wrapped our things quickly together and raced down to the landing. With every boat that came and went we camped a little closer until finally, in nine days, we were first in line.

And when we finally got aboard at dawn, early one morning after waiting by the dock all night, some scowling rascals with pistols stuck in their belts and tobacco juice dripping from the corners of their mouths forced us aside with their fists and pushed themselves on board. Steven was all for a punch-up, but I calmed him down.

The blackguards had already taken the best seats at the front, away from the smoke and sparks and ashes, away from the noise of the churning wheels.

I put my fare, and Eric's (for he had no money), twenty dollars in gold into the hand of one of the sailors who guarded the railing, and we were pushed aboard by the surging crowd behind us.

Steven had decided to throw his lot in with us as well, and so we all three found places by the rail in the back, between barrels of whiskey and molasses. We watched the land shift by slowly, as we glided past, just a hand's breadth above the smooth water of the bay, and then up the Sacramento River. The run to Sacramento itself was some sixty miles. North through San Pablo Bay and Suisun Bay, then meandering with the river as it wove past the mountains that line the coast, finally steaming into the valley set with fields here and there, and on north to the city, where the American River joins the Sacramento and leads to Sutter's Fort.

★ ★ ★

And while we were off to the goldfields, what of the Palmers?

Charlotte Palmer and her husband stayed aboard the *Coventry*, when all the others, myself included, had left.

The captain was not feeling well, and she thought it was just fatigue from the trip. He slept two days and nights, feverish and retching, until she could help him no longer and called a passing waterman to assist her. She paid the man well, in advance as he insisted, and miraculously, he found a doctor and rowed him to the *Coventry* to examine the captain.

"It's the cholera," he said grimly. "I am truly surprised it has not claimed you as well."

There was nothing to be done but try to keep him comfortable. The doctor left her with a vial of laudanum. "It can't do him any harm," he said, "and it might bring him some rest." She paid the doctor the outlandish fee that he asked for—fifty dollars—and he agreed to come back in a few days to check on the patient again. He never did, and she never saw him again, though she stayed in the city the rest of her life.

Captain Palmer lingered for three more days, and when he died, she managed to dress him in his best black suit and sewed him into a cocoon of new sailcloth.

Many of those that perished in the harbor in those early years were unceremoniously dropped into the water for the tide to take. She had seen the bodies of men and animals floating past, and she did not want her husband to be lost like that. So she hailed another boat and paid the two men in it to row his body ashore, and to help her find a place for him near the cemetery of the old Spanish mission. After they had buried him and waited while she prayed for his spirit, she had them row her back to the *Coventry*, where she collected her thoughts and her belongings and found yet another boat to take her ashore again. This time, she intended to stay.

She hired a man with a strong back to push the barrow she had brought with her from the boat to the City Hotel, where she took a room under the gaping mouths of the miners. One wag offered to keep her feet warm for her, offered to pay her handsomely for the privilege. But she demurred, and endured the noise and their gawking stares and made her inquiries. The next day she chose a lot on Second Street, not far from the landing for the Sacramento shipping; she paid a year's rent to the man who claimed to own the land, a penny-pinching scoundrel named James Lick, pitched a tent made from light spars and a jib sail, and started to make her new home.

"I would not go back again to Marblehead," she told me later. "Not without Orie, and not by sea." And by the time the railroad reached the Bay, she had lost the desire to return east with it.

She somehow located several of the crew, two Gloucestermen named Charlie and Vincent, who had used themselves up ashore and never made it to the goldfields. She took them under her wing and put them to work, stripping timbers from the *Coventry* and hauling them ashore, along with any hardware they could use, and the windows from the captain's cabin to mount in front. She painted the facade with the only colors they had on board—white and a shiny black, and even found some wildflowers to plant in front of it.

"So that anyone passing by will know what kind of people live here," she said.

When I returned to San Francisco, she gave me my room and board to help around the place, cooking morning meals and canvassing for boarders. I even discovered a printing press, the same one that had turned out the first paper in the city before the editor got the itch for gold like the rest of us and left for the diggings. I contrived to print flyers for her on it. I met the ships that kept streaming into the harbor and passed out the handbills. At the prices she was asking, she stayed full up, mostly, though many moved on after a few days to one of the newer hotels along Montgomery Street or over near the square, where the gambling halls rolled their music all night.

And now she was expanding the building, trading canvas for wood, wall by wall. She had set up long tables in the shack to feed her lodgers—the tables from our common room on the *Coventry*. More of the ship's sails, painted with designs and numbers, made up the inner partitions for the rooms, and she had sent workmen to strip paneling from the ship to construct the floors, and to fetch the galley stoves ashore to cook on, to take the chill from the tents, and to heat the water for the bath, which she had out back in a little shack. She had carpenters cut barrels in half to make tubs, and it was into one of these Norton sank to wash off the stinking mud that baptized him into San Francisco's ways.

Charlotte Palmer got up before dawn to start the day, hunting for provisions or tending to the laundry, and she never went to bed before ten or eleven at night. She had a bout of palsy not long after Captain Palmer crossed the bar to the other shore, and it left one side of her face frozen in scrutiny, as though she was forever trying to thread a needle. Her brown hair had turned nearly gray in that year, but her heart, if anything, only got bigger and sweeter. Most of the lost souls of the town, young and old, knew they could always get a meal at her tent, and some good advice, and, often a warm dry place to rest for a night. If they were able, she'd put them to work chopping wood or fetching water or scrubbing on some sheets.

I had made the coffee the morning after the Emperor's arrival, and I started on the porridge, my leg stiff with the cold of the morning. Mrs. Palmer was getting the bread ready for the oven, sending little clouds of flour into the air as she kneaded the dough and shaped it into loaves.

"What would you say to the owners of the boat if they came looking for her one day?" I asked her.

"Well, I think I'd just tell them that she disappeared. Do you see any sign of her in the harbor? Besides, they made the cost of this boat four times over before it ever left Boston," she said. "I'd tell them that it's the least they owe me in exchange for Orie's life."

IV

At last the Emperor stirred. He rubbed his eyes as he emerged from his room at the back of the tent. He joined us at the table. It was mid-morning and Norton had slept for twelve hours. I had lent him a suit of clothes while his own were being laundered. The shirt and trousers were much too long for him, but he rolled them to make up the difference. He looked like a waif. I poured him coffee and pushed a plate of biscuits in his direction. He reached for them, but his sleeve fell down, covering his hand. All of us around the table smiled. He was wobbly and still half asleep. He reached for his coffee with his other hand, and the other sleeve swung loose. By now, we were laughing, especially the large woman sitting next to him.

She was the color of dark, oiled oak, with perfect white teeth. Her brown eyes danced when she laughed, and they lit up her face.

"Well, this must be poor Mr. Norton, who fell in a

puddle over his middle and almost never got out again," she said, making some changes in the old kiddie's rhyme. "That was quite an arrival in town, Mr. Norton."

Norton looked at her, speechless, and dropped the biscuit he finally managed to secure onto his plate.

Mrs. Palmer stepped into the silence and said cheerfully, "Let me introduce Mrs. Nancy Pleasant to you, Mr. Norton."

"But... indeed... who?"

"Just call me Nancy, duckie," the Negress replied, and reached out and patted Norton's hand. "Everyone does. If they don't call me 'The Voodoo Queen.' But I prefer Nancy. You look shocked, Mr. Norton, like you've seen a ghost—a black ghost at that!"

The table erupted.

"Indeed, you... well... do... I don't understand. Are you Mrs. Palmer's slave?"

"I never was anyone's slave, Mr. Norton. I was born a free person, like the rest of God's creatures, and always have been. Mrs. Palmer and I went to the Quaker school in Boston together. We've been friends since we were girls. And now God's grace has brought us together again. Fancy that! He surely moves in mysterious ways. And now he's brought you here, too. Whatever can that mean? Mr. Norton, your mouth is still open. Is something the matter?"

"It's simply that I've never spoken with one of your race before. Not like this."

"And they say you're from Africa?"

"Yes, but a white corner of Africa—British, Jewish. You were our servants."

"I certainly wasn't, brother."

"Indeed, indeed. I am awfully sorry. I mean, it was very different."

"You'll need to get used to a lot of new things here, Mr. Norton. Talking to me is just a little one of them."

"Indeed, madam, indeed. But you said they called you a queen." Norton had grown very interested in her. He was over his embarrassment and stared intently into her glowing face.

"Oh, yes, indeed they do. The Voodoo Queen," Nancy replied quite amiably.

"What does that mean?" Norton asked.

"It means that I know about the spirit world. It means that I can call the spirits for good or for ill. Juju power, don't you know."

"You learned this at the Quaker school?"

"Oh, heavens, no! I spent many years in New Orleans where the hoodoo dances down the street. You'd have to be deaf and dumb not to learn anything about it living down there. But you should know about these spirits, coming from Africa like you do, where they come from, too."

"Indeed not. I don't know about powers like that, dear lady. My family were merchants, shopkeepers, at least the family that brought me up was." Norton grew pensive for a moment and then continued, "But there was something strange about it all, as though I didn't belong there and that wasn't who I was."

"Now that *is* very curious, Mr. Norton. Just who would that be if you aren't who you are?"

"Well, it is somewhat difficult to explain. There are some rather, ah, unusual circumstances."

"Never mind about them for now. First let me see your hands, please, Mr. Norton," Nancy said with certitude, and she held out her large hands to receive his. Norton hesitated, then offered them to her. She scrutinized Norton's long, pointed fingers, then turned his hands over, palms up and examined them carefully.

"Ah, yes. I think I know what you mean, Mr. Norton. There is something remarkable here. Look at that line of life, and those mounts of power. Which hand do you favor?"

He replied his right, so she studied the left all the more closely.

"This hand will reveal what qualities you were born with. And the other will tell us what you have done with those gifts."

Nancy Pleasant and Norton were soon united in deep conversation, whispering together over his extended hands which sat on the pillow of his breakfast biscuit. Within a few minutes, they were friends: the Voodoo Queen, mistress of the beignet and etouffée, keeper of secrets, and the Emperor.

V

Norton lingered at Mrs. Palmer's for a few weeks until he could determine where he wished to be. He appointed me as his guide to walk about the city, sniffing out opportunities and learning how things went. I led him to Portsmouth Square, past the gambling houses, which interested him little, and down the byways where many of the few ladies in the city then worked their trade. Norton was not in the least inquisitive about these dens of pleasure either.

For him, it was all business. What was needed in the city? Where did it come from? What could it be sold for? Where did the ones who bought and sold these things live? Where did they meet?

He had helped his father run a ship's chandler's store in Cape Town, and before that, his own business, which had failed, as a chandler in Algoa Bay. He did not wish to return to this same line of work, he told me.

"It's all sailcloth and ashes, my g[ood man]," [he] declared ruefully.

"Why is that, Mr. Norton?" I asked him.

"Well, by all rights, I should not be doing a[ny of this,] not really. Running a shop and all, trading in he[mp and] casks of pitch."

"What do you mean, sir? It's an honest enough l[iveli]hood."

"Ah, but don't you ever think that you were cut ou[t] for something more? Born to higher things?"

"Like what?"

"Well, my mother used to tell me, when I was a boy, that I was really born a prince and given to her and my father by a trusted member of the household of Charles X of France, who fled to England to escape the mobs and assassins. Do you know the Bourbons?"

"Not well enough to invite them over for supper, of course."

"Please don't jest," he reprimanded me. "This is quite a serious matter."

"Sure, they are—or were—the royal family of France."

"Ah, so I am speaking to a man with some education."

"Some," I replied. "Not enough," I added.

"Well, I cannot discount what my mother confided in me so many times. Nor can I forget it."

"I think that many mothers fill their children's heads with dreams like that," I suggested. "It's something to warm you when the days are cold and cruel."

"Nancy has confirmed what I have always felt. She read it in my hands."

"What can the lines of hands confirm?"

"The unique condition of my birth," he replied.

"But, Mr. Norton, surely you must have more evidence than this to make such a claim."

"People have often said," he noted proudly, "that I look strikingly like the Emperor. I have the same nose and eyes."

"The Bourbons are Catholics, are they not?"

"Yes."

"And the people who were your parents were Jews, were they not?"

"Yes."

"Why, then, would these Royal French Catholics leave the last of their line with English Jews?"

"But you see," he went on earnestly, "this is precisely the brilliance of their disguise. Who would think to look for me there?"

We argued on, but he would not budge. Something in his eyes told me this matter ran very deeply in him, like a river flowing beneath the surface calm of the ground and suddenly, unexpectedly, springing up.

★ ★ ★

I continued to help Mrs. Palmer, meanwhile searching for some other occupation to make my way. She urged me to stay on and cook at the Birches. Eventually, I might become a partner in the enterprise. If it offered honest service, good meals, and clean beds, it could only prosper, she predicted. But I found myself talking one day to Edward Kemble, who had returned from the goldfields and was now printing the *Alta*, on the press where I had run Mrs. Palmer's advertisements, and within the week I had accepted employment with him to oversee his shop and to pen stories for the paper. I remained, though, a boarder at the Birches.

Norton was also busy, chatting up the businessmen on Montgomery Street, learning the ropes of the new town. He had met a young man from Baltimore, Peter Robertson, who had some capital and agreed to throw in his lot with Norton on some business ventures. They needed a place to plant their desks.

That evening over pot roast he found out from Mrs. Palmer that the same Mr. Lick who had leased land to her owned property throughout the city, and so Norton went to see him about an office.

In those days, before the papers declared him one of the richest men in the city and he raised a granite building to bear his own name, Lick conducted his business on the front bench of the cart he drove up and down the streets, collecting the detritus that others had left behind in their haste to be off to the mines. The creaking cart was piled high with the culch that washed ashore from the ships. Rags, flattened hats, the remains of animals, bits of tin, bottles, wood, leather—it all got carried back to the yard behind Lick's house, and sorted out, and kept, and one day turned into cash, or if bone, pounded into fertilizer for his pride and joy, the vineyards he had planted in the Santa Clara Valley. But I get ahead of myself.

We found Lick in a rutted lane off Kearney, hacking what remained of a horse carcass into pieces and pitching the fetlocks onto his cart.

Lick was dressed in filthy, torn clothing, and was mumbling to himself as he splintered the horse's bones. "We'll haul you back, now won't we, deario, and we'll put you to rest, won't we, now..."

"There he is," I said. "One of the city's leading citizens. I think I'll nominate him for alcalde in the next election."

"Excuse me, my good sir." Norton approached him.

"Well, now, my good Sir Limey Greenhorn," Lick replied. "What can I do for you?"

He wiped rotten flesh onto his apron.

"I am seeking quarters for a business enterprise that I am beginning shortly with my partner, who has an appointment elsewhere in the city at this moment, and I had been led to believe that you may have a suitable building available for such an enterprise.

"Well, now, lessee," he continued, while with his sharp eyes, he surveyed Norton. "There's the cottage at The Points. That might be right for you. I could meet you there this afternoon about two. Do you know where it is?"

I did and nodded that to him.

"Bring your partner along, my good sir," he went on, "and you two good sirs can look it over."

He had already turned back to his fractured bones before Norton could answer.

JOHN CECH

★ ★ ★

In the grammar school to which I was sent until I was ten, I had a teacher, Miss Capon, who seldom digressed from the lesson at hand. We read aloud from our primers and from Weems's *Life of Washington*, and we studiously contemplated the *Simple Stories for Little Folk* by Timothy Goodwise. I can still recall the first curdled lesson from that wretched text that I was called upon to recite:

The gentleman is a man who has but little to do—who lives upon the interest of his money, and walks about the street. I would rather be an industrious mechanic.

And then we were to cull wisdom from the mistakes of *Fanny Overkind*:

Fanny Overkind, was too kind by half; she thought she could not do enough although being stingy, is a bad thing of anyone, still being a good natured fool is I think much worse. Fanny one day met a poor little boy coming into the house with a basket and asking for cold victuals; instead of giving him that, she went to the store room and brought him down a large piece of rich plumb cake, which he did eat all up; and made himself very sick for he was not used to such rich food.

There were no such epicurean indulgences in our little classroom. We did our numbers as she instructed. We learned proper pronunciation and geography, grammar, and the rudiments of Euclid. It was dry toast for us.

Perhaps that is why, whenever she asked me to recite, I needed no invitation to embellish each lesson with an anecdote I had heard or one which I attempted to fabricate for the occasion. Thus, I would amuse my classmates and myself, much to Miss Capon's consternation. She once spoke with my mother about this habit, and urged her to break me of it—like some wayward colt—since she could not.

"One day his storytelling may take him down a path that he may not wish it to," she told my mother. "Diverting as it is, he should be reined in."

I was shocked to hear of this from someone who defended the veracity of such a bald-faced liar as Parson Weems, who had woven very loosely, as every schoolchild and their parents in New England knew, his tales of Washington from the threads of his own imagination. One has to be very wary of some teachers.

My gentle mother simply shrugged and smiled. "That is his nature, I think," she told Miss Capon. "And I can do little to change it."

I know that my mother liked my tales and always asked me to tell her about each day's adventures at school—a place she had never gone, for adventures she had never had.

Still, I should have listened with one ear to Miss Capon's advice and shown some prudence.

★ ★ ★

"Did you know," I asked Norton after we had left Lick in the alleyway with what was left of the skeleton, "that there is an intriguing story connected with that place he has offered to rent to you?"

I knew I should profess a sudden loss of memory, the Mother of the Muses, and say nothing. Better to permit the man find out for himself and not from me, better to allow another be the bearer of grim tidings, good a story as they might make. Yet I told him—about the tavern that had been in the cottage, and how it had been a favorite haunt of sailors in the city's early days, just a few years ago, but that something always seemed peculiar about the whiskey that Alfie Ellis, the proprietor, served as the evening progressed. Some thought it was simply foul and refused to drink it, others allowed that it was tainted but still powerful and worth the wait. There is no accounting for taste, of course, but these very differences nearly led to brawls several times in the inn. One defended Ellis's potions while another claimed that he was being poisoned by them. Ellis was watering down his drinks, to be sure, and in the end he became engrossed in the effect that the water was having on the whiskey and his customers. He decided to investigate the well, and he lowered a lantern, only to find a skull staring up at him from the surface of the water. In went a grappling hook, and piece by piece brought the remains of a sailor's body up with it.

Charming.

Enough, I thought, to send anyone flying in search of better quarters.

But Norton did not seem at all affected by my tale. "I am not interested in the water," he said. "Or the local legends."

And that was that. He and the polite Mr. Robertson, a sober Presbyterian, met with Lick at the cottage, agreed on a rent for one of the rooms with windows that let them keep an eye on the busy harbor and a nearby dock. Norton was in business—Joshua Norton & Company, General Merchants.

He quickly left the Birches and moved to one of the hotels near the square, and then to another, and finally to the Jones Hotel on Samsone Street, right in the thick of things.

He and his partner bought and sold cargoes—sugar, beans, coffee, potatoes, pickax handles, nails—anything that might be traded in the city. They even acquired a boatload of cats from Mexico, which they sold for ten dollars apiece to butchers and bakers and restaurateurs throughout the city, to decimate the ranks of rats. And like Lick, Norton started buying up lots here and there. Within a year he owned three of the four corners of Jackson and Samsone Streets, on land that had just been filled in with ships' hulls and garbage and sand, and in a few months more, there were buildings on the land and he was renting the buildings.

He had the Midas touch, they said. The water lots that he bought off Rincon Point had come with an abandoned ship, the *Genesee*, that still had sound holds. Norton had the vessel's masts removed and its hatches secured, and he used it as a floating warehouse. It came in handy because of the fires that had been sweeping through quarters of the city every six months since Christmas Eve of 1848.

Everyone knew the fires had been set by the Sydney Ducks, a gang of cutthroats from the penal colonies of Australia, escaped or exiled to California, and given a second or third or fourth chance in the gold fields. But these lads were not bred for handling a pick or shovel— oh no. They cracked the heads of drunken sailors and emptied the pokes of the celebrating miners back from Angel Diggings; they terrorized the ladies of the evening and snatched what they desired; and they disemboweled Chinese and Chilianos just for the sport of it. When pickings got lean on the streets, they lit fires and watched everyone run while they looted the shops, the gambling halls, the tents, the banks. You had to be careful not to wander even a few blocks north of Portsmouth Square, into Sydney Town, just below Telegraph Hill, the land of Billy Sweet Cheese or Bungaraby Jack and their chums and their wicked ways, lest you find yourself in pieces in the Bay.

Norton and Robertson lost their office in the May fire of 1851, when seven million dollars and more of the city's property, the cottage on the cove included, collapsed in flaming ruins. But Norton took it all in stride. I met him on the street and he commissioned me to put a notice in the *Alta*, stating that he was still in business and where he could be reached.

"It's nothing, my good man," he said. His new black frock coat was flecked gray from the ashes that were still falling on the city. "Please remember me to Mrs. Palmer when you see her," he added, tipping his hat and hurrying off for an appointment somewhere.

He was a man of some property, a man of growing civic importance. And they wanted his hand on the charter of the San Francisco Committee of Vigilance when the city's leaders decided to become the law and start hanging any Ducks they caught. Norton had even put his name to their compact and allowed his picture to be taken for their secret files. The daguerreotype still exists, I believe. Norton in his evening suit, his face framed by muttonchops, tight-lipped, looking sideways, uneasy, at the camera.

"It is appalling that any country should submit to such ochlocracy!" he exclaimed to me when we next met. "Bad as they may be, these men deserve to be heard. Why, if I were emperor . . ."

"Norton," I said amiably, "you are talking about scoundrels and reprobates who would slice up someone's guts for bootlaces without thinking twice about the matter."

"But that's not the point. Even the murderer deserves a hearing."

"Well, then," I responded, "why have you added your signature to the list of executioners?"

"You're not supposed to know about that."

"Everybody knows, my friend. Everybody knows. The committee is even giving out membership diplomas for people to frame and hang on their office walls."

"Well, it's business. I'm not proud to say it, but there it is." He had that worried look that he sometimes got when his body was here, but his mind had journeyed elsewhere. "I cannot really rent out space on the *Genesee* to people who have been burned out and not stand with them on this. Besides, I'm not a citizen, and I'm from the same empire as the Ducks. People will say I'm siding with them, and there goes my reputation in a puff of smoke."

"But I didn't think you were worried about that, your majesty," I dug at him.

"Well, of course, if I had my titles and all, I would not have to be, but I do not, and so I must scratch like all the rest."

So Norton had watched John Jenkins, that careless Sydney safe stealer who was caught in the act, hung from the rafters of the Customs House by the committee's sheriff. That man of the law would be the famous Captain Ned Wakeman, who had the fastest ship in the Bay, the *New World*, which he had just managed to spirit out of New York Harbor the year before even though the vessel was impounded by the local bailiffs, one of whom he took hostage so as to make good his escape. Captain Ned treated the waterfront like his private fiefdom. He was not famous then, of course; Sam Clemens saw to that later. Mostly, Ned was bluster and bully and bravado, floating on barrels of spirits, taking chances only when they were certain to reimburse his reputation.

But Norton's sense of scruples were bothered by the whole affair. The next time they caught one of those Sydney rascals, a highwayman who went by the sobriquet of English Jim, Norton stood up in the meeting and demanded that the suspect at least be allowed to speak on his own behalf. He had to shout down the crowd to do it, and it was an act that was not without courage, but he eventually persuaded them that fairness meant that at least Jim should have his day in court.

"I'll second that," Norton told me someone said. "Let 'im speak and then we'll hang 'im."

Once again, Captain Wakeman did the honors, this time from a davit on the Market Street Wharf. And later in the summer, there were two more of the Ducks, friends of English Jim's, already in the county jail, who were dragged out of jail during Parson Williams's Sunday service for the prisoners. The crowd pushed them down to the committee's offices on Battery Street. The men knew what was going to happen and dug in their heels to keep from being forced into the stairwell and up to the meeting room on the second floor. It could not have been more than ten minutes before Wakefield appeared in the window, waved to the crowd, and announced at the top of his lungs, "Here come a couple of Satan's boys from Sydney—we'll send them back down under!"

The crowd cheered.

Then, one by one, for he had prodigious strength, Wakefield threw each man from a window like children's playthings. They were caught up short by the ropes that were tied to the beams above. You could hear their necks snap like dry twigs. With a thousand others I witnessed the event, for it fell to me to write the story for the paper—those blue tongues, the excrement streaming down their legs, and all the church bells of the city madly ringing.

Norton was nowhere to be seen on that occasion, nor on any of the others when the committee meted out its justice. He did not have the stomach for that. He took no delight in any of the cruel games some denizens of San Francisco played in those days, like setting a terrier loose in a packing crate of rats to see how long it took for ol' Trey to liquidate the vermin. Nor could any business obligations persuade him to witness the fights in the old Spanish ring that pitted a tormented grizzly bear and a frenzied bull for the entertainment of the crowd. Nor could he partake in other famous sports of the city, gambling and whoring, or abide the assaults on foreigners. That was the specialty of the Hounds—the same crowd from Sydney who claimed to have reformed with time and now were doing the community the favor of cleansing it of undesirables. One night we had met on the street, and watched—helpless to do anything about it, it occurred so suddenly—as a pack of these monsters drove two Chinese, their long braids trailing behind them, into the square and beat them senseless to the pavement with sticks, then robbed and kicked them again before the game was over and they disappeared back to Sydney Town. We sent for a doctor and the constabulary at once, but it was too late to help these poor men. Norton was so shaken by the event that I had to guide him to his rooms.

★ ★ ★

Most frequently I encountered Norton at the theater, where he loved to go. I saw him in the audience for *The Bandit Chief*, at its first performance in Washington Hall, and at Dr. Robinson's Dramatic Museum, when the new hall opened on the Fourth of July in 1850. They did Dr. Robinson's *Seeing the Elephant; or, Seth Slope's First Visit to San Francisco*, a howler about a green Vermonter that had every Yankee in the crowd bouncing his knees on the floorboards with joy. It was followed by Mr. Evrard playing a cloddish fellow who tries his hand at an oration and gets everything topsy-turvy, then a twirling Scottish fling with bagpipes, and for a finale the doctor's "Used-Up Man," which he sang with rueful mirth, a testimony to the condition of many in the hall that night, who poked their neighbors in the ribs and nodded knowingly when they heard:

O I ha'nt got no home, nor nothing else, I s'pose,
Misfortune seems to follow me wherever I goes;
I come to California with a heart both stout and
    bold,
And have been up to the diggins, there to get some
    lumps of gold.
    But I'm a used-up man, a perfect used-up man,
    And if ever I get home again, I'll stay there if I can.

By the time he got his character to the diggings and back with nothing in his pockets, there was not one there who did not think this was his song:

I don't know what do, for all the time I'm dodgin,
To hunt up grub enough to eat, and find a decent lodgin;
I can't get any liquor, and no one seems to meet me,
Who'll take me by the collar now, and kindly ask to treat me!
    For I'm a used-up man, a perfect used-up man,
    And if ever I get home again, I'll stay there if I can.

Myself among them.

VI

Back in my bed at the Birches that night I sang myself awake with my own chorus of that song, about what used me up and left me beached again in San Francisco, with a leg that will scarcely bend since Sacramento and the North Branch. I know it all by heart, like a pilgrim knows his beads, and though I know the ending, know every grief and pain, know I will not sleep that night; still I repeat it once again, counting every step of that journey.

★ ★ ★

It was seven in the evening by the time Eric, Steven, and I arrived in the city, and we were able to disembark. We searched for a hotel along the front street, but all the shacks and tents were filled with men like us heading for the diggings.

"Go over to Sutter's Fort," one of the innkeepers advised. "It's not far. They'll accommodate ye."

We had all heard of Sutter, on whose land the first gold was found. But we did not expect to see what we did on the hour's walk to the fort. The land had been stripped bare, ruined. Bloated, rotting bodies of horses and cows lay beside the path. The crops were trampled in the fields, bushes were torn to pieces to make fires by the army of scavengers that had been through this countryside, taking everything it could use on its march.

Sutter's Fort was a long, high-walled building, made out of adobe bricks, with a sturdy gateway that was now flung open to the night air. People came and went at all times of the day and night, heading to the goldfields or returning, unloading merchandise, or readying a wagon for the camps.

Within, the central courtyard was ringed by little shops, stalls, really, where a few farmers displayed their vegetables and where one merchant, Sam Brannan, had a large store of goods neatly stacked and ready: tins of oysters, jars of pickled cucumbers and beets, matches and percussion caps, knives and pistols, powder and ball for the older weapons, flasks of whiskey, pans, picks, shovels, sacks of beans, sugar, and coffee—all at prices to make your eyes roll.

Hitchcock's Boarding House was on the second floor of the building that sat in the middle of the courtyard, but it was full up by the time we arrived, so we found some space next to the wall and camped there the night. We got little sleep. Conversations swirled around us, like leaves caught on some swift current. An old man in a battered suit paced the plaza in the fort, chatting with people we could not see. It did not matter. We were close now and so restless to be on our way we did not even talk.

At daybreak, cooking fires hissed, and we treated ourselves to eggs and ham with slices of bread, washed down with coffee so hot it blistered your tongue. Five dollars each for a meal which we would hardly have paid a tenth of for, back home.

Then we tried our hand at horse trading. We bought a horse and a mule, both of them well worn and ill fed, for the princely sum of one hundred and fifty dollars—nearly all of what I had left. We knew we'd been swindled and Steven began to say so, but I quickly replied that we'd easily make it back, and much more, once we got to mining. Besides, how else were we to carry out all the gold we found?

"Yessir," said the drover, who had the animals for sale, "you'll probably be wantin' a wagon for the tons of ore you'll take out, right enough. But ol' Maggie and Horatio here will see you through till you can get one of them rigs."

"How'd a mule get a name like that?" Steven asked him.

"Ain't you never heard of *Hamlet*?" the drover asked back. "'There's more beneath heaven and airth, my dear Horatio, than yeve dreamed of in yer philosophy!' Sweet lines, those. And every time I look at that mule I remember them. Now I'll have to get some new ones."

The drover showed us how to load our packs on Horatio and gave us some directions for the Russian diggings.

"I don't recall seein' any of them the last time I was up in the north, but that don't mean they ain't there. Just be careful crossing that stretch of the river—unless you-all kin swim."

We followed the path north from the fort along the south side of the American, which led to Sutter's Mill where those first grains of gold turned up in the sluice. Tiny flecks they were, the biggest no larger than a kernel of rice.

Maggie was a slow, plodding horse, skittish at the sight of a hand, and we took turns riding her. Philosophical Horatio never looked up from morning till night and was surefooted even on a bad trail, and there were plenty of them.

All along the way, we could see the work of miners. On the bends, where the river currents built up bars that could mean gold, deep gouges had been cut into the sand. The dirt was thrown up on the banks, or farther down the stream. And then, just below a place they'd named Big Bar, we saw groups of men—as many as a half dozen in each—dumping shovels full of dirt into wooden contraptions that they called cradles. They doused the dirt with dippers of water and furiously rocked back and forth to get the gold to settle out on the bottom. Some others at Big Bar itself had a long trough, set on an incline, that they loaded with dirt on the top. Then they washed down the soil and looked for gold in the cleats on the bottom. This we learned was a Long Tom.

"You can move a lot of dirt this way," one of a bunch of miners from Ohio told us when we stopped to rest and talk with them. They were doing fine, so far, getting a steady twenty ounces a day from this dig, enough to meet their expenses. But you never knew when it would play out and you couldn't keep yourself in beans.

"Now who be you?" one of his comrades asked us, with a little suspicion, from the side of his mouth that didn't have a pipe in it.

We told them, and said where we were heading.

They were friendly again, when they knew we wouldn't be living next door. They even let us camp with them that night and shared some of their deer meat with us.

"I don't know about any Russians, or them from Peru or the Chilianos, or the yellow fellers, or any of them. Ya oughta be stickin' with yer own. Them's the boys you can trust out here," the one with the pipe said, looking at Eric. His tobacco smelled like burned rope. "If you ask me, ain't none of them should be diggin' here anyways."

"Where would you go, then?" Steven asked him.

"Well, I can't rightly say," he replied and stopped poking at the fire for a moment. "Some say you should go here and others say there. But if I was just starting out like you fellers, I'd go where they haven't dug up the riverbanks yet. Farther up in the mountains, where all the gold begins."

★ ★ ★

We left with first light and kept as close as we could to the river so we did not lose our way. A few miles above Big Bar we passed through a camp of Negro miners. They were very friendly, gave us coffee with chicory in it, and told us the best place to cross the river was a morning's walk farther north, at a place they called Forksville.

They had several Mexican women living with them. These were the first women I had seen for many days. They hid their faces from us under their shawls and retreated into their tents.

"Mind that mule in the water," one of the Negroes said. "A mule in the water can be a funny thing."

Our crossing later that morning was not without event, but Horatio was blameless. Maggie stepped in a hole and threw Steven into the icy water. She quickly got her footing back, but Steven lost his dignity. Although it was a hot day, he shivered through it until his clothing dried.

We passed through Forksville, which was just a few sad tents, and continued up to Horseshoe Bar, where there were many tents, a few cabins, and polite company. They were doing well from their diggings. They were Mormons who had gone on west from the Great Salt Lake to explore California, to see if the land might make a proper home for them. They found gold instead, and were socking it away for the church.

"It was an angel led us to this spot," one said, and the rest nodded. "And he's brought you as well, no doubt.

Join up with us, and the church, and you'll be saved, and your parents and their parents too, even to the beginnings of your generation."

"We'll have to think about it," I said warily.

"Do that," he rejoined. "Think about it, and join us."

They invited us to stay on and try one of their claims, offering us half of everything we found. They showed us how to pan in the river and gave us a place to work. By day's end, I was seeing spots from the heat of the sun and shivering from the cold of the river, and poor Steven had taken to the shade.

"Bricks is one thing," he gasped. "But they ain't this never-ending misery."

Eric kept right on working, and it was he who managed to earn the most that day.

We stayed with the Mormons for a week, thinking it over. Steven made about twenty dollars for all his efforts, I made forty-one, but Eric cleared a hundred in scale gold, those tiny flakes that you must wash out of the sand, and in two nuggets of several ounces each, which he dug from the ground with his knife, as he picked his way to bedrock on the riverbank. Eric had the touch, they said, and they pleaded with him to stay on and bring God's goodness to them all. They would find a wife for him, or even two, good Mormon women if he would only join them.

"Sank you," he responded politely while he patted the poke sack around his neck that held his gold. "I go mit mein frendz, sank you."

★ ★ ★

The river branched again at a place they had just decided to call Auburn, after the town in New York State, which was the birthplace of Bradford Pease, the Methodist parson who ministered to the miners from his tent with the flaming cross painted on it. Pease had been in the Sandwich Islands, bringing the Good Word to the natives, when he heard of the gold. Many of his converts had already left for California and so he decided to go along.

"I believed there would be many souls for me to save here," he told us when he joined us after supper around our fire. "Most of the Kanakas were coming here to work for Sutter on his lands, and then to mine for gold, so I just did what our Good Shepherd would have done and followed my flock."

"But how did Sutter find them and why did he bring them here?" I asked. "Oh, now that's a story," Pease said as he eyed the pot of beans we had left on the stones that circled our fire. "It would be a pity to let those beans go to waste, would it not?"

"Help yourself," Steven offered.

Pease settled in with a spoon and the pot and told us Sutter's story, how he left his family penniless in Switzerland in order to come to America, where he worked on the Missouri frontier, gathering every scrap of knowledge he could about the West from trappers, traders, mountain men. Then he made his move and headed for California, in 1838. He ended up in Fort

Vancouver with nothing to tax his ambitions. Bored, impatient, he took the *Columbia* to the Sandwich Islands, with his dog Beppo—you know, the yellow dog that smoked a pipe. There it was he raised the capital for his expedition to California, which belonged to Mexico in those days. Sutter arranged with his confederates in Honolulu to have several hundred Kanakas sent to slave in his fields and father his children, that old fornicator. All for the glory of New Helvetica, which was what he named his lands. What presumption, from a conniver and debaucher! In ten years he had more land in his name than any other single person in this whole country. Until the gold. After that, there was little left that he could call his own anymore, and all his loyal subjects from the islands were panning for their fortunes on the American.

"You saw them on your way here, did you not? At Lacey's Bar, just below us?"

We had—the solid, dark-skinned people in their conical straw hats, men and women alike, washing out baskets of dirt in the water. Singing together beautifully.

Had Pease heard of the Russians?

"Well, the Russians, you know, have been here since before Sutter. And even though they say they are a Christian people, they can act like heathens if you ask me. I've heard a lot about the healers they have—drive away illness with charms and chanting, and spit liquor on your head to ward off evil spirits. I don't know where they may be, but I hope they stay far away from us. I have enough trouble trying to keep the Kanakas from spending all their gold on American whiskey without having to contend with the Russians as well."

★ ★ ★

We pushed on the next morning. Pease was already at his claim. God and gold, to his mind, were not incompatible. "The Good Lord put it here," he told us. "It would be a sin not to accept his gifts."

By afternoon we were alone on the river without any other settlements around, no sounds of other miners, no sermons, not even a bird song.

It was hot. We tied Maggie and Horatio in the shade and took our tools to the river, where we could see a little sand bank on a slight curve. We panned the afternoon away, standing in the cold water, and earned about two ounces for our labors.

We spread our camp under the trees near the animals, who chomped contentedly on the grass and underbrush. Then awful noises interrupted our sleep. Growls and snorts, and then whinnying and braying from Maggie and Horatio. Steven produced the five-barreled Colt that he kept in his belt, and I fished my derringer out of my jacket pocket, and we went to see what had become of the animals. They were gone. Something was thrashing in the bushes nearby, and then it reared up. A snarling brown bear, huge, the kind they call grizzlies. Steven fired three times at its stomach. It roared, slapped an angry paw in the air at Steven, and left us, lurching into the woods. We called for the animals and looked for them most of the next morning, but we never saw them again.

I persuaded my friends to leave that unfortunate place and push on up the North.

We split the weight that Horatio had carried. About fifty pounds apiece. It was hard going along the river, rocky and tangled; at times we waded in its current because the banks were too steep or overgrown to permit us to pass.

Three days of this. Steven's shoulders and mine as well were raw from the packs, so Eric volunteered to take some weight from each of us.

"In za armee, I carry many more pounds zan zis." We could only marvel at the good cheer he kept with double the load.

Two more days. Hot days, cool nights, blisters and sore feet. Steep hills rising behind us. The twisted arms of trees swinging in the moonlight against the dark sky.

We decided to rest for a few days and regain our strength. We scoured the woods around the river, and up the hills behind the woods, looking for anything we might eat. Berries, mushrooms, anything. Eric trapped a rabbit on the second day and I made a stew. We drank the last of our coffee and ate the rest of the beans on the third. We found wild berries that day too, but they only made us sick.

I thought we might die out there.

On the fourth day, we heard voices coming down the river from above our camp. One of the voices belonged to a tall man with reddish brown hair. He wore a shirt buttoned up the side, with fanciful embroidery around the collar. His shirt was cinched at the waist with a large belt into which he had thrust several revolvers and a knife. He had a rifle over his shoulder, and a light pack with a metal flask jangling from it.

His companion was an extremely short man, not even five feet tall, and round as a barrel. He carried two rifles, with belts of cartridges crisscrossing his chest. In the belt around his middle he carried an ornate curved dagger in a silver sheath. He had the deeper voice, and he seemed to be scolding the taller man as they walked into our camp.

Another man followed these two, not much taller than the short man, but thinner, and dark-skinned. He had the eyes of a Chinese, slanted upward at their ends, with a thin beard that outlined his mouth and the cheeks of his broad face with its weather-lined skin. To ward off the sun he had tied a piece of cloth, knotted for fit at its four corners, atop his head. His outfit consisted of a vest, trousers, and shoes made of animal skins, sewn together like a crazy quilt.

His pack was even larger than those of his companions, and like them he was well armed. But he had his rifle at the ready in his hands, and his watchful eyes saw us long before his companions did.

In fact, the crane and the barrel (for that is what they resembled) were deep in conversation, which they finished, in a language we had never heard before, all whispers and sudden stops for your teeth and little hills to make with your tongue on the roof of your mouth. Then they turned to us, as though it was the most natural thing in the world for them to have found us there.

"Vell, good day to you, sirs," the tall man said, taking the cap with its shiny patent-leather bill from his head, and sweeping it with his arm into a bow.

"I am Nikolai," he proclaimed heartily and smiled. "This is Grisha," he continued, referring to the barrel, "and this is Serdu. We are at your service."

We had found the Russians, or they us. They had been hunting bears, and debating at the same time the proper method for curing the meat. I doubt they would have gotten within a league of a bear, unless he was deaf, with the noise that they were making.

They immediately comprehended our condition and insisted that they help us back to their camp, a good afternoon's walk farther north along the river. We could barely manage the march, but they were very kind, and waited for us to catch our breath, and gather our resources for the steep parts of the path.

At last they led us into a small sheltered valley, where they had strung up large pieces of canvas between trees to block the wind and made of these a kind of courtyard. In its center a fire burned always, with tea in a pot made of brass atop a tall metal urn of a type I had never seen before, but later learned was called a samovar.

Some thirty souls composed their camp, most of them Russians, but a number of others as well, blown to this place from around the world, all living there in harmony. In this group were several Kanakas (happy runaways from Parson Pease's fold), four Negroes from Kansas who came overland together, a Chiliano student, two Mexican brothers who had grown up in California, a reindeer herder from the land of the Sammis, a painter of holy pictures from Thessalonika, and a father and son from Cathay, who made extraordinary pots from the clay of the riverbank.

Most amazing, among the Russians were also five women and, even more remarkable, two children, a baby boy, Sasha, and the other a little girl, Katya, about three. Nikolai's family. His wife, Masha, tended to them with great pride and pleasure. The children were dressed in spotless clothes, the baby in white, and the little girl in a colored skirt with deerskin boots that her father had made for her.

The whole encampment doted on the children, and the miners all were careful to wash before they offered a callused finger to the baby or pushed the little girl on the swing they had built for her in the clearing among the arbored tents.

Nikolai and his family, and the other Russians who had joined them here in the hills, had come, bearing letters of commission from the Tsar, across the straits from Siberia, where they enlisted Serdu and several other master woodsmen of his tribe to join them on their exploration of the coast below Sitka. Nikolai had moved inland to the valley, where they planted orchards, grew wheat, trapped. But this life was quickly changing, with the gold and statehood on the way, and so many immigrants. Land was bought and sold with little regard to who had honest claims to it. Their only interest, Nikolai explained to us, was to dig enough from the riverbanks to secure their future in the valley, in this paradise. What shame for them to have to drag themselves back up north or, worse, across the sea again, with only their belts to hold up their pride, to be laughed at by the relatives who said they should not ever have gone to this heathen land.

We were given a place near the fire, in a tent that was temporarily vacant. Masha carefully folded and tucked away the belongings of the owners in the corners and placed the sacks of gold they had left behind on top of these piles, unhidden.

And we were fed like princelings. Bear steaks (which I understood were provided by Serdu) and fish, a delicious mush made from roots, sweet wild strawberries, tea and honey, and a powerful clear liquor, distilled from potatoes, with which they toast every morsel.

Nikolai and Grisha cooked the bear steaks together, arguing about how long they should remain on the griddle, arguing about what the weather was going to be like that evening, arguing about where they should dig next, arguing about who should accompany them.

"We always fight like this," Nikolai told us in the nearly flawless English that he had learned from the Hudson Bay traders up and down the coast. "But we never fight when we sing, this Cossack and me. Once we can agree on a song!"

The evening drifted away for me with these songs, some rollicking gay ones that had everyone clapping, others melancholy. Grisha could rumble a deep bass and then soar up three octaves to do a high, perfect falsetto. Nikolai played a small triangular guitar with dizzying speed, and Nikolai's brother, Dimitri—Dima —wheezed out melodies on a small concertina. The last words that I remember hearing that night, I later learned, went:

> *Coachman don't drive the horses so*
> *For I have nowhere, nowhere else to go.*

We were full and happy and besotted.

★ ★ ★

They worked the bend of the river that fronted the camp, and spread out in expeditions of smaller parties to prospect the little streambeds, now dry in the summer, that wound into the hills of the Sierra Nevadas and fed the North Fork.

There was a constant coming and going of smaller groups. Upon each group's return, there was a prayer to the Virgin and the Child, an icon painted by the artist in the camp and displayed in a small shrine on its eastern side. A meal followed, washed down by glasses of their fiery drink, and then, for dessert, the news about the luck the group had had on this "finger" or that "arm" of the river—the Russians spoke that way.

They willingly shared their hardships and their good fortune equally, and this bound all the parties here together. The gold was divided into even shares, and the sacks were left quite openly by their owners in their tents, as had occurred in ours, even while they were away at another dig. They agreed upon their plans together, and I am sure they would have given the children a vote in the conduct of their camp's business had they been able to express their views. I had sat many times next to my parents in the meetings of Hancock town back East, and listened to the proud, perdurable debates that decided the slow and steady course of life in our village. But I must say that what I found here in the wilderness of California was the truest expression of our great democracy, for it respectfully included all, without regard for sex or nation, age or color, genealogy or the contents of one's purse. From the moment I was among these people I felt, at last, that I had truly found a place I could call my home.

The work along this portion of the river was steady and productive—an ounce a day, sixteen dollars, for everyone who worked the Long Toms that the Russians had built from hollowed-out logs. Occasionally, they would uncover nuggets in the ditches called coyote trenches they had cut to reach bedrock, where gold was often found. One of the biggest of these was the size of a small plum, and they gave it to Katya to play catch with.

That was only one of the wonders that filled this camp. Theodoros the Greek had traced ancient designs on the outside surfaces of the tents and filled their interiors with handsome scenes of his native countryside. Always, on the eastern walls of the tents he painted holy figures and tableaux: David, Jonah, and Daniel in the Lion's Den; Christ dividing the loaves and fishes; Angels ascending and descending their heavenly ladder while Jacob sleeps and dreams.

We were served tea from small green cups that Qu Yang fired in a stone oven he had constructed at the edge of the clearing. The cups he passed to me had cracked in the kiln, and so he filled these fissures with molten gold. From a flaw, an accident, he told me quietly, can come a thing of rare beauty.

★ ★ ★

As soon as we could travel and work, we each went out with a different group. I agreed to join Grisha and one of the Negroes, tall, thin James Mulberry, on a trip to prospect farther north into the mountains. They were hoping for that big strike, the mother lode, that might make the fortunes of us all.

We took a mule for our provisions and walked nearly two days from camp along the river before we turned from its course, up a steep little gully and followed it for about a mile, testing the soil to see how rich it might be. For some reason no one had been up this "finger" before.

James was all for going on. "Yah knows, Grisha, this ain't much. We kin come by here and root aroun' on the the way back."

"Nyet, nyet, nyet!" Grisha exclaimed. "Iss sumsing about ziss place. Ve say dis in my peeple, 'God iss not vitout His mersee, and da Cossack iss not vitout hiss luck.' Dats me, da Cossack."

★ ★ ★

The next day we began to dig and pan—dry diggings, they are called, when you don't have water to wash the sand and soil away from the gold. You have to fling the contents of your pan into the wind, letting it carry away the lighter soil, leaving (if you caught well) the gold in the bottom of your pan. James was a master at this, and though I tried to acquire his facility, I kept getting clouds of dust blown back in my face.

We reached bedrock quickly, in less than two feet. And even I caught well that day. Before long we began to build a pile of nuggets and a cup full of flakes. We saw some of the nuggets resting against the granite when we scooped away the gravel, and we could scratch them out the rest of the way with our knives. By the end of the day, we calculated that we had drawn nearly fifty ounces from that streambed—about eight hundred dollars' worth. And the next day was just as good, indeed better—close to a thousand. We kept working the bed, up into the hills for nearly a week, till we were at the end of our provisions, and we had close to twenty-five pounds of gold which we carefully funneled into three cloth sacks that once had held our coffee and flour.

Grisha was full of song as we left the valley. We had replaced the dirt as best we could and scattered the ashes from our campfire. At the mouth of the valley he had me climb a tree to mark it with a notch high enough so that it would not be easily noticed by another prospector coming up the river.

"Vee vill come back for ziss," Grisha asserted. "And ve vill make a claim."

"Grisha," James told him, "I'm a-changin' my mind about you and yer luck."

We started late and so only walked a half day back down the river, Grisha warbling at the top of his lungs, and James adding a line when he could.

We camped for the night on the riverbank.

Some time after midnight, we awoke to find five strangers in our camp.

★ ★ ★

"Well, now, lookee here," said one of them, the one with the beat-up hat. "What'ave we got here. A nigger and a fat little ferriner and it 'pears to be a Yankee."

"Looks like we just found us a little luck," said another in an old army tunic stripped of its insignias. He pointed his rifle at us, motioning us to raise our hands, while his confederates went through our gear and found our gold. They untied the mule and began to load the sacks of gold and what they wanted of our gear onto it. Unexpectedly, James was in motion, crossing the clearing to try to stop them.

"Now just you hold on there," he said.

But before he could take another step, or say another word, they overpowered him, beating him to the ground with their rifle butts, while the one with the battered hat unsheathed his knife and plunged it into James's neck repeatedly, while the blood poured from his wounds and his head rolled back and sideways, nearly severed from his shoulders.

The murderer wiped his weapon on James' shirt and his accomplices watched our friend's death throes with merciless satisfaction. Grisha quietly drew his own knife and then, with a roar, hurled himself at James's killer. He buried his long blade deep in the breast of that devil, and placing both hands on the hilt, twisted the knife in the wound so that it was sure to take its full revenge. The others surrounded Grisha and clubbed him with the stocks of their rifles until he collapsed on top of his victim. He moaned once more, and they hit him again. Then one of them drew a revolver, placed its barrel next to Grisha's ear, and pulled the trigger.

Then they remembered me.

"Now what about you, Yankee," the one with the pistol spat at me. "Whatcha reckon we should do to you? Your friend there just stuck Freddie through the heart. Mebbe you should pay for that. Mebbe we should string you up from one of these trees and take you apart piece by piece, dontcha reckon?"

Before they could reach me, I kicked the ashes from the fire in their faces, and ran the few yards to the river and dove in while they shot at me. It wasn't too deep that time of year, perhaps four feet, but its icy surface hid me for those few seconds, and I swam downstream until my lungs cried out for air. When I came up, I saw them on the shore, aiming at me, so I gulped and dove again, this time heading for the opposite bank and a group of rocks that I thought might offer shelter.

We played cat-and-mouse for half an hour—longer it seemed to me—until one of them said, "Ah, shit, let him go."

"But he seed us," said another.

"Who's he gonna tell, Henry? He ain't got no boots, no food, no nothin. If the bears don't get him, the snakes will."

"I ain't gonna let him get away," said the one named Henry, who kept watch on the bank.

I waited till a cloud covered the moon and eased quietly out into the stream. My hands were already numb, and my right leg throbbed with pain where one of their bullets had hit me. I kept my head in the water and floated, paddling with my hands under the water, twenty, thirty, forty yards downstream from him; took another breath and floated further. The next time I looked, I was a hundred yards away. But the moon was out again, and Henry was beginning to follow the current downstream too, where he knew I would be going.

So I floated and drifted, trying to keep ahead of him, which I somehow contrived to do, despite the cold and fatigue that had set into all my limbs.

Still, he followed, for another quarter hour, till his friends, now mounted on their horses, called to him. He took one last look and shot his rifle in my direction. It landed closer than even he might have guessed, just a few yards away.

I waited for the sound of their horses galloping away. Instead I heard them fording the river, and when I peered around the rocks where I was hidden, I could see that three of the men were riding down the side of the river I had fled to, while Henry walked his horse along the other.

They searched both banks for some time, and by some miracle, I managed to stay underwater, in the shadow of the rocks until they had passed, though I thought they would surely hear my teeth chattering each time I had to come to surface to breathe. With the horses splashing, and the men talking back and forth across the river, they missed me.

Then Henry crossed a quarter mile farther downstream, and they were gone into the brush and trees.

And into my darkest nights.

I pulled myself up onto to the bank and shivered beneath some bushes and left my senses. When I awoke, it was morning, and I was wracked by tremors and a searing heat in my leg. I could see then that I was wounded badly, above my knee. When I moved the leg, it hurt so it made me retch.

I do not know how long I lay there.

In the afternoon, I was looking into Serdu's face, which he crinkled into a smile, and then proceeded to pour that fiery liquor into my mouth.

"Wodka goot. Drink you. Much."

My head began to reel. But he had me drink still more.

Next, he looked at my leg, and before I could say anything, he sunk his knife into my flesh, probing for the bullet, and swiftly pried it out before I lost my senses yet again.

When I awoke, I found a poultice of mud and leaves pressed into the wound and held there with a strip of my trouser leg.

Serdu loaded me onto his shoulder, crossed the river, and then carried me along the other side. He walked through the night, setting me down long enough for him to rest a little, chew on some smoked meat he produced from a pouch on his belt, and draw deeply from a flask of water. The liquor he reserved for me.

I fell into a stupor again, and next remember shouting all around me.

Little Katya's face hovered over me.

★ ★ ★

They brought the bodies back and buried them with ceremony in the hills behind the camp.

I heard their laments, the wailing among the Russians, the deep whispering songs of James's companions.

I shook and slept and dreamed of Mount Monadnock, that I was climbing it again, as I had done the last fall before I was sent away to Chandler's. I dreamed of the colors in the valley spread below me, and I dreamed that I was passing through the clouds that crowned its summit. Now light was everywhere around me, and my poor body was left behind there in that tragic camp. An old woman I had not seen before chanted over me. She bathed my brow with a fragrant cloth, singing the same few notes over and over again. I knew she was calling me and I did not know if I wanted to return.

They sent me down the river to Sacramento with a Serdu in a bateau carved from the trunk of a tree. Eric and Steven stayed behind. I told them what I knew about the diggings we had found. They could look me up in San Francisco if they ever got down there. I would print or cook, do something, anything but dig for gold again. To get me started, Nikolai gave me my share of what they'd earned since I arrived in the camp. They waved to me from the shore. Nikolai held his little son in his arms, while Katya stood quietly next to him. He was surrounded by family and friends, but he looked grim and alone.

In Sacramento, Serdu deposited me on the dock that served the steamers that ran to the city. It was late October and trees all around us were turning golden. A few leaves shook free in the crisp breeze.

"How will you get back up the river?" I asked Serdu.

"Paddee paddee like crazee," he cheerfully told me. Then he pointed to the rope he had coiled in the stern of the boat and said, "Moizetbietz pull like crazee man."

He had liked the feathered charm from Rio that I still wore around my neck. When I was recovering, he said, "Serdu lisen za bird hin fezers ven fetch mister hom. Hit sing much."

I slipped the cord over my head and pushed the charm into Serdu's hand and wished him farewell.

Without even glancing at the city, he cast off, turned to wave, the charm in his hand, and with deep, graceful strokes of his paddle was soon lost in the shipping and then in the bend of the river.

★ ★ ★

Leaning on a stick, I limped aboard a new ship on the run, the *Mercury*, captained by a loud gangly waterman named West, who was trying to make his name on brag and a fast boat.

With winter approaching, the currents of humanity now flowed away from the placers and the mines and back to the city. Some snow had dappled the higher peaks of the Sierras, and the fall promised to be very damp indeed. Serdu had somehow explained to one of West's crewmen about my injury, and so I was let aboard. I was lucky to get a seat.

The *Mercury* lived up to its name. We were in San Francisco within eight hours, enough time for Captain West to have as many rum punches with the grizzled miners that had struck it big up on the Yuba or the Feather—it didn't matter which, since both rivers had been picked clean. They were bringing sacks of gold back with them, and West gave them the royal treatment, which they paid for, of course. Fifty dollars each, I heard, for their private cabins. The tins of oysters were extra. West's first mate docked us—the skipper himself was too blind to see.

Something had changed about the harbor. Several

new wharves shoved their planking into the water. Many of the ships were now lit up. Their crews had not returned, I later learned, and the vessels were being used as floating hotels by enterprising sorts who had simply taken them over. Other boats had been hauled ashore, where they became gaming houses or hotels. The *Niantic* was one of these, a terrible place that smelled of rot and disaster. Another, the brig *Euphemia,* had been left afloat just off shore—there was talk of turning her into a prison or a haven for those who had been parted from their reason, which might have described a good portion of the city in those years. The *Panama* had got religion and they were saying Sunday services on her, and still other vessels had become warehouses. The frigate that washed up at Pacific and Davis had been transformed into a restaurant trumpeting Giuseppe Bazzuro's Spaghetti. Those with vaunted tastes liked to add, with a smirk, "con rodento."

I looked for the *Coventry* but did not recognize her among the hundreds of vessels, in various stages of salvage or decay, that were still anchored in the harbor.

The town had grown. The elves had been busy in the night, it was that changed. Pixilated. But the buildings were quickly and cheaply built. Among them were a host of the new "portables," made from corrugated iron —that brown metal—hauled all the way from New York or even London.

New buildings facing the harbor had sprung up along Montgomery Street, and off to the west, on Portsmouth Square, you could hear the orchestras of the gaming houses prancing through their melodies. Sharp polkas to keep the blood dancing and the bets flying. They were all still tents then, the El Dorado and the Bella Union and the California, but within the year they'd be framed in, snug and tight, along with several hundred others, from one side of the city to the other.

And there were other tents everywhere—tacked onto the sides of shacks, and pitched on their own in the soggy ground—for the rain had indeed begun already. People trickled back to the city from a summer at the placers, to pick up their old jobs again, or to start new businesses and find other ways, like the old man from Oregon said to me the first day I was ashore, to help the gold hop into their pockets.

The porch and the City Hotel were both still there. I turned left and headed slowly for Happy Valley, where I thought I might find some friendly faces. I'd heard from someone on the *Mercury* that many Yankees were living there.

I had to thread my way through the wagon ruts and the refuse that covered the streets. The stench from the roadways and the harbor was horrific, and many tied handkerchiefs saturated in pleasing scents around their noses and mouths to ward off some of the smell. Merchants had begun to fill the holes in front of their stores with anything handy—barrels of spoiled tobacco and sacks of flour filled with weevils, old packing crates, horse dung and old shoes, broken tools and rotten vegetables. A flattened piano sat in a particularly large crater, mixed in with forgotten melons and the carcasses of dead horses and rats as big as cats and dogs. But it was impossible to keep ahead of the rain. The holes would stay treacherous for another year, time enough to give the Emperor a chance to arrive in the city and fall into one of the worst of them.

Happy Valley remained a sea of tents that turned, at nightfall, into magic lanterns strung up the hillside. The shacks and small wooden buildings that had been built made use, like Mrs. Palmer's, of lumber from the ships; native wood was far too expensive still for these everyday uses. Sutter's Mill would have supplied enough boards for the entire city, but it was never finished and sat for years in the ruin of that first goldfield, like the bones of an ox plucked clean by vultures.

I was hoping for a place to stay with other people from New England, but it didn't matter. I asked a fellow in a yellow hat if he knew of such a place, where a Massachusetts man might feel at home.

"Try over yonder," he said, pointing to a shack that had hung a ship's stern window next to its white front door. Above the door, a sign read in large letters THE BIRCHES, with a picture, in black and white, depicting a grove of those graceful trees. A long tent was stretched behind the wooden section, the canvas of the tent painted to look like wood as well. A ship's bell was hung next to the door, for the visitor to ring, which I hastened to do. The door opened, with a smell of fresh bread and fried onions, and there stood Mrs. Palmer.

These strings of memories are woven through our minds. I have tried to understand and guess their pattern, without great success. On this particular evening, like all others since these events took place, I could only watch with anguish and wonder while these threads were spliced once more on their noctural loom, and hope near morning for the kindness of sleep.

VII

As his star began to rise in the city, I saw Norton as everyone else did, on his daily promenade late in the afternoon along Montgomery Street.

Out being seen.

Out seeing who was doing well, who was sporting a diamond stickpin or an ebony cane with a gold ferrule, who might need a broker on a consignment of two tons of nails.

Norton most assuredly had the constitution for business. On the three corners he owned of Jackson and Sansome, he had a cigar factory, a rice mill, and a third building let out to other businesses. His water lots rose spectacularly in value when the Pacific Mail decided to build a terminal next door and rented storage space from him. He moved in grander, ever higher circles. He no longer had to worry about the well beside Lick's cottage or the portable that replaced it after one of the fires set by the Ducks. Norton was now in a granite building on Battery Street, No. 110, where people the likes of Sir William Lane Booker, the British consul, had their offices, and Occidental Lodge Number 22 of the Freemasons, Sir William's lodge, invited Norton's membership.

Norton resided at the very respectable Rassette House and dined with the McAllisters, gracious Hall and snobby Ward, the social arbiters of the city in those days, and their cousin Sam Ward, gourmand, lover and supporter of the arts, friend of Longfellow, and brother of Julia Ward Howe, who penned "The Battle Hymn of the Republic." All three had come west for the business of gold, and they included Norton in their orbits, introducing him to one Bill Sim, a giant Scotsman, who was seeking a partner for a variety of ventures. Norton's old associate, Peter Robertson, had had enough of the elephant and was returning East, so Sim bought him out and joined forces with Norton.

It was then that Norton the aristocrat earned the nickname of "The Emperor" around the McAllisters and their friends on Pike Street, because he invariably fell into the unwavering line of discourse that America needed a strong, absolute hand to rule it out of its unruly ways.

"What this country needs is an emperor, that's clear," Norton was likely to add to almost any discussion on nearly any subject. Take what happened to come up on this particular evening after dinner: the need for more and better-manned fire companies to respond to the conflagrations that raged through quarters of the city with ferocity, taking everyone and everything in their paths.

"And why is that, pray tell? Will an emperor help put out a fire?" Ward would bait him, sipping on his port.

"Well, of course," Norton would respond seriously. "At least in a manner of speaking. He can levy the taxes to take such necessary measures for the public good, without waiting for people to volunteer. He can insist on better building regulations. He can single-handedly throw out things like those metal portables, which bake alive everyone who happens to get caught in one of them during a fire. And he doesn't have to wait for legislation to be passed. He can act, and act boldly."

"Norton, you are a true monarchist," Sam pitched in. "Whatever could have brought you to this country?"

"Yes, and what could possibly be keeping you here?" Ward added, as he languidly puffed on his cigar and arched his eyebrow for punctuation.

"Well, he is an emperor without an empire," Hall replied. "Like most of us here. Even old Sutter lost his. A mob of prospectors has a funny way of digging up an empire. It seems like the only empire one can rule over nowadays is named for a saloon or a hotel."

"Yes, but an emperor has other things to be responsible for," Norton persisted quite earnestly. "The moral tone of a place, for example, and public decency. These all flow from a worthy emperor. Justice, fairness, equality, too."

"Why Norton," Sam interjected, "you're sounding more like a Minuteman than a Tory. Stick around, and one of these days we may even turn you into a proper Democrat."

★ ★ ★

And Norton now was partners now with Judge Lansing Bond Mizner, buying up lots together on North Beach from Alderman Henry Meiggs, Honest Harry.

That's when the trouble started.

And it started with a handful of rice.

There was a shortage of rice in the city, and it was selling for thirty-six cents a pound, up from a paltry four cents only a few months before. But there was no rice to be had. China was suffering famine and forbade any of its rice to be shipped abroad—least of all to this land of barbarians. Even if it was called Gold Mountain.

After a supper of baked salmon with new potatoes, a spinach salad, and a custard tart topped with slices of fresh apricots, Norton was fed a tip by a friend of the McAllisters', Willy Sillem, that a ship full of Peruvian rice was waiting to be unloaded from the *Glyde* once the weather cleared and she could be wharfed. Norton and his partner only had to come up with the $25,000 for the cargo, $2,000 down and the rest in thirty days. Norton took a deep breath and made the deal.

Within two days, two more ships were in the harbor, and they were also loaded with Peruvian rice. Then another came, and another. Rice dropped to three cents a pound; Norton tried to get out of his contract claiming he had been tricked into buying a boatload of rotten rice. The Ruiz brothers of Peru, the owners of the rice, sued. The jovial Scottish colossus, Norton's partner Sim, left town, and Norton was ruined. It was December of 1852.

But the end did not come quickly. The case dragged on and on in the courts for two and a half years, with Norton winning one round and losing the next, back and forth until the final ruling against him in May of 1855.

One by one, Norton's properties disappeared. He tried to rally, call in favors and find a toehold, somewhere. He formed a business venture—a stock brokerage firm—with a lawyer and member of the state assembly, Isaac Thorne. It evaporated in a few months. He turned to real estate, but that was a bust. He lobbied for the nomination for County Tax Collector, even though he was not a citizen and could not run for public office, even though he had claimed—to the McAllisters, their friends, and anyone else who would listen—not to have any confidence in democratic government. He moved, twice, to less expensive quarters. He lost his membership in the Masons because he could not pay his dues.

The boom years were over. After the first fortunes had been made and spent, the ones that were to be amassed now were those in politics, banking, and large business firms, not in property speculation or panning gold dust from the rivers. The single miner had drifted back home, or down to Australia, or up to Oregon, or to the other side of the Nevadas in search of the next placers. The mining companies bought up the claims and hosed down the riverbanks with pressurized water and hired burned-out miners at five dollars a day to pan the dust. They sank shafts to bedrock and pulled out the gold mixed with quartz, and set up mills to grind away the crystals. It was complicated, and it demanded money to accomplish.

Political scandals and sagging property values plagued San Francisco. Honest Harry Meiggs, the alderman from whom Norton and Mizner had bought their lots, absconded with city funds and city records. His development scheme for North Beach collapsed, taking with it a number of banks and several million dollars in city funds and numerous smaller investors, spreading a lack of confidence throughout the area and plunging the city economy into its first depression. It nearly bankrupted San Francisco, and would have, too, had the city not decided to simply disavow the debts.

As if this weren't bad enough for the city and its future Emperor, Norman Bugbee, an architect and friend of the McAllisters', charged Norton with embezzlement. Bugbee had left his investments in Norton's care when he traveled back East in 1852 and upon his return wished to see the books. Norton put him off and went to the bank to raise the money to cover what he owed Bugbee and salvage what he could of his reputation.

He sat across the desk from a wiry former soldier turned banker, a Captain William Tecumsah Sherman, who had served in the army in California under Mason and who would serve again under Lincoln in not too many years. Sherman squinted at him, ran his hand through his short red hair, and asked Norton what collateral he had for such a loan.

"Well, Captain, there are the water lots at Rincon Point. They're worth a tidy bundle."

"Were, Mr. Norton, *were*," replied the captain and lit a cigar. "Nothing's worth what it used to be. You're a Jew, are you not?"

"Well, I was raised a Jew."

"Then you'll have a good nose for this sort of thing."

"But I don't think I really am a Jew."

"Why not? You appear to resemble one."

"Ah, but I also look like someone else," Norton went on.

"Who would that be?" the captain asked, curious now.

"If you would take a moment to peruse this, please," Norton said, offering him a coin.

"What is this?"

"A French franc. From 1828."

"Oh, Frog money. Knowing them, it's probably counterfeit."

"But look at the figure on the coin."

"Yes. It's one of their kings."

"It's Charles the Tenth, last of the Bourbons. Now, look closely. Now, look at me." Norton turned his head so that the Captain could regard him in profile.

"My God," said the Captain. "Was he a Jew, too?"

"No, no indeed," Norton responded, and out fell the

story. He informed Sherman of his mother's confidence that he was, in fact, a Catholic prince wrapped in a tallith. His title—could he ever claim it, and he produced papers to show the Captain that he had taken certain steps abroad to secure the unimpeachable proof necessary to do so—would stand as his collateral. "And grant this orphan his rightful paternity," Norton added.

"Do you know that I was an orphan as well?" remarked the captain, who had the reputation in the city for his garrulousness, and offered Norton a snifter of brandy.

"When my father died, our family was left destitute, and a wealthy friend of his, an attorney named Thomas Ewing, agreed to take one of us boys and raise him as his own and make a proper man of him. My mother said, 'Take Cump,' for that is what they called me, short for my given name, Tecumsah. 'Cump is the smartest of the lot.' So I was sent to this chilly family. And do you know what the first thing they did was? They baptized me a Catholic and conferred on me the name of William so that my first name would not be that of a pagan Indian chieftan."

They talked the afternoon away and in the end settled on a loan that would pay off the debt to Bugbee and spare Norton any more court embarrassments.

"This is for your honor, sir," the captain told him with bonhomie as he ended their interview. "And may I suggest that you find a new line of business now that you've been properly skinned?"

Later, when Norton failed to make payment on the

loan, the water lots went to the captain's bank, Lucas, Turner & Company.

Norton cobbled together something of a life for the next year or so, acting as a runner between merchants and bankers who once had made bargains with him, taking his handshake as a guarantee. Mizner, the McAllisters, and all the rest had dropped that hand like a hot skillet handle.

VIII

The next time I saw Norton was January twelfth of 1857. He was sitting on the end of the Pacific Street Wharf at midnight with a pistol to his head.

The noise of our boat and the light of its lanterns stopped him. He glanced at us, lowered his pistol, and stared blankly into the harbor. My companions shipped the oars and secured the Whitehall to cleats on the wharf and, before they were done, I had leaped from the boat and run the few yards to the end of the wharf. I could see in the flickering light that the pistol had returned to his temple.

"Please, Norton, don't. Wait!" I had pulled up short of him and now approached him slowly lest some sudden move should set off his weapon.

He did not resist when I carefully pointed the gun in the air and then removed his finger from the trigger and uncocked the hammer. It was one of those older revolvers, not one of the new Colts.

My companions hallooed me.

"Aw, why dontcha let him end his misery?" said Gus Harn, one of the watermen who had rowed me over to Oakland. I was writing a story for the *Bulletin* about the fire there earlier that evening in the shipyards. "We fish 'em out of the bay alla time. It's a mercy for the buggers."

"You know," my colleague Randolph Johnson observed, in his imperious way, "if you save a soul's life, you are responsible for it. Now do you want to take this mendicant home?"

"Go back to your doodles," I told him. He was the paper's artist and would have to provide the drawings to illustrate my story. "Think of this poor soul when you're scratching those hellish flames we just saw on your pad. Think of yourself, man. Wouldn't you want somebody to stop you?"

He shrugged. "Not if I truly wanted to be leaving this infernal town."

"Go ahead, you wretch. I'll be along."

They saluted, turned, and left me with my old acquaintance, who had nearly set himself adrift in eternity.

He had changed a great deal. He was nearly bald on top, and deep lines creased his forehead. His shirt collar was smudged with soot, his dark coat was stippled with dirt and debris.

"Norton, you are a sight. You look like the chap in Dr. Robinson's song. Remember? We heard it together. Remember:

> *Oh, ladies and gentlemen, what shall I do?*
> *I'm an object of pity, I'm certain, to you—*
> *I'm all out of cash, and I'm out at the knees,*
> *And nothing sticks to me but flour, mud and fleas.*

I even did my best impression of the intrepid doctor for him, hopping on my good leg. But still he didn't budge. In fact, he cocked the pistol again.

"Norton, remember who else we saw?"

I was talking fast now. Trying to summon up better days, some reason, however flimsy, to give him pause, and me a chance to wrest the revolver from his temple.

"Remember we heard Mademoiselle Lucienne sing "The Spirit of California" at the Jenny Lind before it burned, and remember Mrs. Baker, her Julia in *The Hunchback*, you said you were transfixed by her. Remember how you blushed when you passed her later on the street. Remember how she stirred you up, you said?

"And of course, of course, how could I forget Lola Montez, beautiful Lola, darling of King Ludwig, Dumas, Gautier. Now who wouldn't fight a duel for her, drool on her slippers, fill her bath with lavender, towel her off with rose petals?"

I was warming up to my task.

"Remember we paid five dollars each at the American to see her do the Spider Dance, and we didn't know what we were looking at, it seemed like she was trying to get pepper out of her clothes or to stomp some bug on the stage. Remember how she married—a sad day for us all—and how they moved on to Grass Valley, and how she held court there and walked her pet grizzly through town. Remember the riot she almost started in Levee City, and Miska Hauser had to play his fiddle to calm that audience, they thought all that leaping about was a hoax.

"And Norton, remember your favorite—Miss Anna Maria Quinn, not quite seven, who did *Hamlet* at the Metropolitan. I know, it's true, she didn't do the whole play, but remember what a prodigy she was? Did you know Ned Wakeman heard her first on the *New World*, reciting some scenes when she was on her way with her parents from Sacramento to San Francisco? He got her to perform that very day on the afterdeck. In my opinion, it was the best thing that old windbag ever did for the city.

"Remember how she did little Eva and we all were bleary-eyed, and the next week she did Little Pickle and had us howling in the aisles. And remember how she just up and vanished to Tasmania when they found gold down there?

"And remember Billy Birch and Eph Horn? Ethiopians my eye. Billy played the bones—remember, his were ivory with golden tips—and Eph made himself sound just like a steam whistle, and remember how everybody waited for "Tobacco Jake"? Remember the part that went:

> "*When I was young, when I was young
> I used to saw de log,*

> *And wid ole Gumbo, all de day,*
> *I've salted down de hog.*
> *I've steered de raft, I've dug de clam,*
> *And drinked dat good old rye*
> *Which dat old gemblem, Uncle Sam,*
> *Still drinks when he am dry."*

"Now that brought the house down, and remember how they made him sing it over and over again until he smiled and shuffled himself backwards off the stage?"

I did the song for him then and there, hoping it might bring him back to this world. He chuckled in spite of himself, and then he wept.

IX

He was spent and it was late. But I lifted him to his feet and started to walk him, like a drunk, and the only way to bring a drunk to sobriety is to burn the spirits off through the souls of his feet. I walked him up Telegraph Hill past the Heliograph, and down the other side to North Beach. Little by little, he told me everything—about the lots, Bugbee's funds, the shame. We ended up at Abe Warner's at the start of Taylor Street, near the water where Meiggs's wharf would have been if his scheme had matured, close by John Denny's.

They started calling Abe's place the Cobweb Palace a little later, but it was already well on its way to earning the name when Norton and I stepped down the stairs from the street and entered the double side doors.

A monkey stirred from his pallet and slowly came over to us, his thin little black paw held out to beg for a peanut or a penny.

Other animals and birds shifted in their cages. A green parrot with a long scarlet tail called out from his perch on the bar as we entered, "Aaaawk, Grandfather, hands on deck, hands on deck. Aaaawk, *por mis santos timbales, mis santos timbales.*"

"Quiet, Pedro, quiet, you old bag of execrations," said the man behind the counter. "Did you know, he can spew maledicta and confusion in four tongues?"

That was Abe. He never seemed to leave or close the premises, and he never seemed to change out of his black frock coat, his long white apron, and his tall opera hat. He had a brown beard then, streaked with some silver but it would turn to snow white with the years.

"Perdio santo a le bocie! a le bocie!"

"What's he on about now, Abe?"

"Something about blessed God's bowling balls. Shush, Pedro, don't be going on about God like that. Shush, shush. Quiet, you bag of green farts. He was left here by an Italian captain, who had him from a Russian, who had him from a German, who had him from a Cuban. He's been around the world more times than he has tail feathers, and all he learned from it is how to swear."

He'd smoothed the bird's feathers, scratched him behind his head, fed him a piece of biscuit and calmed him.

"Awwwk, Grandfather," the bird cooed to him.

Abe was from down Maine and he knew chowders, crab cakes, and toddies like no other. He set up there, near the end of things, when he arrived in 1856, and stayed on that spot, filling it with animals that were left him for safekeeping and never retrieved, or that he bought for a dollar or two because a sailor needed to keep on drinking. He'd loaded shelves with scrimshaw carvings from the sperm whale crews, with talismans and amulets, cryptic stones and effigies to bring luck or disaster to their owner—a shrunken head from Borneo, the twisting tusk of a narwhale, a bull's pizzle, a gallery of naked majas, road signs, campaign posters, and portraits of ships tossed at sea, a lama's prayer wheel, a Saracen's slipper. It all found a place to settle, somewhere, in Abe's until every inch of the rooms were filled, and still he kept adding. Nothing ever left—though in later years he was offered enormous sums to part with certain treasures that had been bestowed on him in recompense for an evening of hot gin laced with cloves.

Nor was anyone ever shanghaied from his place to fill out a crew for a boat bound for Constantinople or Siam. He knew all the press gangs and crimps and wouldn't let them near his bar. This was a safe harbor.

Abe was watching a spider weave her web in the lamplight, running her threads back and forth between a post that ran through the bar and up to the ceiling and a battle club from some savage island of the South Pacific.

"We can learn a great deal from the spider," Abe mused.

"And what might that be, Abe?" I asked him, propping Norton up next to me at the bar. Abe knew me from my work at the paper. I had written up a story about his establishment a few months after it opened, and sung its praises. From time to time I ended up here at the end of a long day, chatting with Abe, or more than likely simply watching the spiders with him. I had tried his crab cakes, served with a sharp red sauce, and found them sublime and told him so.

"Patience," he replied, scratching his beard. "And diligence. You know, a spider is a great deal like a human being. It spins a web, someone comes along and tears it apart, and it just goes back to spinning another. But a spider is not like a lot of the humans I meet here because it does this without complaint. It doesn't screech about its religion, and it doesn't need a philosophy. It just gets on with its work. I admire that."

"We could both use one of your toddies, Abe. My friend Norton, here, has been through quite a time."

"Yes, I've heard about your troubles, Mr. Norton. Read about 'em, too," he replied knowingly, as he set about fixing our drinks.

"Abe, maybe you could help us. Norton needs to find a way out of his financial fix."

"Well, for starters he should not be purchasing any more rice." Abe chuckled.

Norton squirmed.

"I'm sorry, Mr. Norton. Just a joke. You know it's pretty late. Keeps me awake. I'm sorry. I can see you're worried sick."

"That's not the half of it, Abe." I was standing behind Norton, and so I made a sign behind his back—put a finger to my temple and rolled my eyes. Abe caught my drift.

"Here you go now, drink this up, Mr. Norton. It'll warm your bones while I think a little." Abe looked at me, then studied Norton's face for a long time in the same way he had looked at the spider and its web.

Norton and I sipped the drinks, though it was all I could do at first to get him to take any of it down. He hung his head listlessly and only at my urging lifted the mug to his lips. Finally I got one cup into him. The monkey was sitting on the bar next to Norton's hand; it tugged on his little finger, and Norton began to gently pet its head. It climbed on his shoulder.

"You know what I long for?" he finally said aloud. "I would like to see my dear father, I mean my stepfather. He would know what I should do. I did not see him again before he died. Oh, if only I could talk to him now. He would know."

The clay mug Abe served his toddies in felt good against my cold hands. The cloves and lemon in the drink gave the musty air around us in the bar a comforting fragrance of something rich and wild growing here among the sand and the rats and the suffering. We could make out raucous voices coming closer down the street, the sound of oaths and glass breaking. The animals began to move in their cages again, restlessly, as though they sensed a storm coming, and then the voices drifted past our snug cove.

"Well, there is no easy answer to your plight, Mr. Norton. But I know of someone you should meet. She's just come out here a few weeks ago, from back East.

She's from Maine, actually, which is how I know her. My wife's cousin, Eleanor Dunster. She is giving a demonstration tomorrow night at the Auditorium about something they call Spiritualism. You have heard of the Fox sisters?"

Who had not? Everyone in the country who had read a newspaper in the last five years had followed the story of the girls, Margaret and Kate, who heard noises in their house in Hydesville, New York—rappings, they were called. The spirit of a peddler was trying to communicate with them, and once they could decipher his knockings, they learned to their horror that he claimed to have been murdered in their house by a Mr. Bell, the previous owner, five years before the Foxes had moved in. Most of the village bore witness to these rappings and testified to their veracity. In fact, the villagers themselves had joined in the interrogation of the peddler's spirit and helped elicit this information from his responses to their questions.

Word of Miss Dunster's appearance had already spread quickly through the city. There was a buzzing about her, brought on in part by the notices that she placed in the *Bulletin* concerning her demonstrations, and added to by word of her powers. Rumor said that she was a true clairvoyant. She could see things that were invisible to the common eye, see to the heart of things. Even Randolph, my cynical colleague, had gone to sketch her for the paper and could only celebrate her beauty and her charming candor.

Abe went on. "Miss Dunster can also talk to spirits,

and they reveal many things to her. They are aware of matters we do not know about ourselves. They can lead us to the past and to the future. Maybe they can tell you something that will help you. This a pretty hard town, and we need all the help we can get. She's an honest and good young woman, and very sensitive to anything that is out of balance. And you, Mr. Norton, if you don't mind my saying so, are a little out of balance tonight."

X

I took Norton back to Mrs. Palmer's, where I continued to board, and where he was heartily welcomed. She had lost two buildings in the fires, but she had managed each time to build a bigger, better house the next time.

"It's the only insurance I can get," she confided in me. "More rooms and nicer rooms. That way I can make something extra just in case the Ducks get loose again with their damned torches."

She still lived at the edge of Happy Valley, but farther back from the harbor, where some semblance of a neighborhood had begun to form. She had never remarried, though suitors frequently offered her their hands, including Theodore Hightalling, the carpenter from the *Coventry* who had gone to the diggings and returned to San Francisco with eleven thousand dollars' worth of gold dust. He began to build houses in the city and prospered. He even built Mrs. Palmer's house on

Howard near Fourth, stopping by to supervise and to take over the trim work. He barely needed a ruler, he could measure every stick with his eye and he was seldom off by more than a whisker. He hardly spoke, except to grumble a retort while his thick fingers flew delicately over the boards. He was a joy to watch—a fine workman always is. He remained unmarried, but he faithfully called on Mrs. Palmer every day.

There are too few real friends in this life, and we need to remain near those that we have. And so I stayed close to these. They sustained me in the turbulence of San Francisco as I was recovering from my ordeal and then establishing myself as a printer, with the *Alta*, as I have said, and later with the *Bulletin*, and as writer for these and others.

Mrs. Palmer gave me a special rate for my room, since I still helped her with advertisements and referred good people to her. She often cared for young women who were cast adrift in the city, and the children who washed ashore with them or alone at her doorstep. At present, there were three youngsters in her house, sleeping on cots in her room; she tidied them up and fed them, and if they were old enough, she put them to work helping out around the house. She told them stories and taught them the alphabet and tended their colds, and later she found families in town that would take them in.

I gave Norton my bed and slept on the divan in the parlor downstairs. He was hardly a drinking man, and so Abe's toddy had made him quite tipsy, even after the night air and the walk back across town. I knew he would sleep without hurting himself. Besides, I had his pistol.

The next morning we collected his things from the rat hole of a hotel where he had been staying and moved him into Mrs. Palmer's; she gave him a room back by the kitchen. It was really little more than a storeroom, but it was the only space she had, and since he had scarcely any money, it was the most that he could afford.

"Back East they used to call the room off the kitchen 'the dying room,' because it was warm there and the ancient ones liked it," Mrs. Palmer remarked when she and Norton spoke over lunch that first day. "You had better not be planning to die on me, Mr. Norton."

★ ★ ★

That evening we arrived early at the Auditorium to hear Miss Dunster, but the benches in the hall were packed, especially since she did not charge admission for her lecture. There were still so few women in San Francisco that I suspect many of the men in the audience came to gaze upon her.

She was a young woman, perhaps no more than twenty, with light brown hair which she arranged tightly behind her head. She was dressed entirely in black and displayed only a small white lace collar and a silver brooch at her neck.

She stood beside a table, bare save for a glass and a pitcher of water, and explained in a careful, measured voice the substance of her belief and its practice.

"I discovered," she told the curious crowd, "that from quite a young age I could communicate with the spirits of those we call the deceased. They are not really dead, however, they have simply passed over to the Other World. These spirits are willing, nay, eager to relay their messages to us, if only we are prepared to listen with all sincerity. This is not as remarkable as one might think. Part of us is spirit, and it has never joined the corporeal world at all. Does it not make perfect sense for it to return to an immaterial world when it is free of the body which contained it? These spirits can reveal much about our loved ones, and they can sometimes tell us about the future and how best to prepare ourselves for it. I am simply their medium, a channel through which they tell their story."

"I hope you're a deep 'un," someone shouted from the back of the room "or we'll all get stuck on you!"

The unruly one was prodded into silence by his neighbor, and Miss Dunster smiled placidly and went on without perturbation.

I cannot pretend to understand all that she said, about the migration of souls, or the place these spirits reside, the heavens and hells of their world. They sometimes spoke to her by rapping out their messages, like some kind of celestial telegraph, if you could read the code. They sometimes chose to write their notes on paper through her hand, and at other times they dictated poetry to her fingers.

"I do not know the manner in which this music of the spirits will come," she said. "I simply try to play it as best I can when it does."

She would be available for consultation with individuals after the lecture, in the hope that she might in some way help some people in the hall to speak with their loved ones over the distances of space and time. She did not charge a fee for her services, since it would be an affront to the spirits, and she was not interested in and would not ask them about material things—where a treasure might be found or which investments would yield the highest profits. If they wished to tell us of those things, it must be entirely of their own volition. However, she would gratefully accept any gifts that those she was able to help might bestow upon her, since she could not spread the word without some modest resources.

"Why doesn't she ask the spirits to chip in?" a wag in the back grumbled.

"She sure is purty," an old miner in his best overalls and jacket offered. "But what she's saying doesn't hold as much water as a handkerchief in a thunderstorm."

I must say I was not skeptical. Our house in Hancock had been one of the oldest, and we were not the first family to live in it. Before my father built the big barn behind the house, the animals were kept in the stalls that had grown out of the first house and were attached directly to it behind the kitchen. We still used these rooms for storage, and my own room was above them. Late at night, when the farm was quiet, I could often hear the sounds of horses being led into their stalls below me, their hoofs crashing against the wooden partitions between them, and the shouts and calming words of someone bedding down the animals. I know this was not the voice of my father or brother playing some trick on me. I told my gram about it. She nodded and said, "That must be Henry Butler, who had this house before us. The house is talking to you, son."

For his part, Norton was quite enraptured by her, and he insisted that we speak with her afterwards. It took us an hour before the people who had crowded around her with questions thinned enough for him to approach her. She was putting on her bonnet and cape and turned her face, with a serene smile toward him. He kissed her hand.

XI

Two evenings later, Norton had me in tow as we hurried up Market Street to Miss Dunster's rooms at the St. Francis Hotel. We were shown up to the second floor where the door was opened by an older woman, Miss Dunster's mother, we later learned, who indicated that we should join a group of nine others already seated around a large table in the center of the sitting room. Miss Dunster smiled with beneficent kindness at my companion and then began what she referred to as her séance.

Except for the two candles on the table, the other lights in the room were extinguished and the curtains tightly drawn.

"Please join hands with your neighbor on either side," Miss Dunster instructed. "This will form a chain of energy that has power enough to call the spirits. If you wish you may close your eyes and concentrate on calling them. This too will help."

We did as she invited, and I must say that, after the general skittishness around the table had subsided, I felt a curious tingling running through my hands. I thought it might be fatigue, for I had been hard at work all day in the composing room. The chamber had been close when we arrived, but now a cold draft suddenly swept over us, though I am sure no windows or doors were opened.

Miss Dunster went around the table, calling us each by name and forging the links in the chain, she said.

"We must all be united in this," she continued evenly but firmly, to Mr. Jones the banker and Herr Strauss the cloth merchant and the others assembled, "if we hope to have such intercourse with these spirits."

Behind each of us, Miss Dunster could distinguish a form, an aurora of light that was invisible to our unskilled eyes, and in this light a loved one lingered. She did not wait to hear rappings on the walls or floor. She moved quickly from person to person, looking intently at them, quickly surmising a message from the spirit which she relayed to the loved one at the table. We learned that wives and children were well, that aged parents endured or were lost at Christmas to the ague, that one orchard thrived and a barn was infested by boring beetles, that a favorite horse had to be put down, that a partner was, indeed, not to be trusted, that Mr. Fisher's family was in dire straits since he had left them, and that the dead father of Miss Fair, the only other woman present at the table, had not suffered in his passing to the Other Side, and he blessed the union that she sought with the young man Joseph Frank, who had recently asked for her hand in marriage.

"Your father is smiling, Miss Fair. He is playing with a brown-and-white spotted dog and smiling."

Invariably, the recipient of each message was caught by surprise. Some dissolved in tears, others shook their heads in amazement. There was no possibility that Miss Dunster could have known about the substance of their lives in such detail; surely they had not told her. Then she gazed intensely and for a long time at something, or someone just above my right shoulder.

"Your mother is here," she said to me. I had not asked Miss Dunster a question, as others had. She continued, "She has dark hair streaked with gray and wears a blue dress with little yellow flowers to trim it. She worries about you, you know. She believes you may be too trusting and easily misled. 'Always honor your own spirit,' she is saying to you, 'and do not do anything to trammel it. Follow your best lights and they will always guide you well.'"

Now it was my opportunity to be stupefied with the others by the uncanny accuracy of Miss Dunster's words, for my mother often had said such things to me, and I felt her close presence in the room, and my eyes filled with tears.

When Miss Dunster arrived at Norton, she suddenly stopped her rapid progress around the circle. She stared for some time at the phantasm that surrounded him, and then, unexpectedly, her eyes rolled back in her head and she began to rock from side to side in her chair.

"What is it, Miss Dunster?" Norton asked her, his voice choked with apprehension.

"I see a crown," she said, nearly in a whisper, "and a scepter, no, a staff. They are yours if you choose to take them. Your father is giving them to you. He is dressed in resplendent clothing and sits on a throne. The things he offers you are rare and extraordinary. He knows what you are searching for. He has something to say to you, '*Cherchezpourlalaclalacdorlalacdorlalacdor.*' I do not understand these words. '*Cherchneznequittez-pascherchezpresquelecapdeniegenequittezpas.*' Ah, now he holds his hand aloft to salute you."

"What can this mean, Miss Dunster?" Norton said, when he sought her out later, after the others had questioned her more closely about their loved ones' messages and slowly departed from the room. As they left, they pressed coins and bills, even a bag of gold dust into her hands, which she in turn conveyed to her mother. I put a five-dollar gold piece into her mother's cool palm. Norton gave Miss Dunster his watch on its golden chain, one of the last things of real value that he possessed.

"These Spirits do not lie or mislead us," she replied. She seemed older than her age and fatigued by the undertaking. "If they urge us to do something, so we should."

"But what is it I should *do*?" Norton asked, his voice rising plaintively.

"First, I think you should attempt to fathom the message," she said to him in her calm, even voice.

"I think it is in French, Norton," I interrupted. "I've

heard enough of it around the city to know its sounds. I've written it down as best I can remember, and I know who we can ask."

Norton thanked Miss Dunster profusely and excitedly bowed his way out of the room. Soon we were on our way to a small restaurant that I knew, in an lane off Bush Street, run by a Frenchman named André, who had come to San Francisco from Paris on the lottery the government had held to send the poor and the troublemakers to California. He was one of the former, and one franc had changed his life.

"Ah, my old friend," He greeted me warmly and escorted us to a table in the back. "Eet has been manee months, no? You still scribbling for ze journal? Attend a mineet, and I vill return."

He made a circuit of the tables and then was back at ours.

"Now, what do you desire, messieurs?" he asked.

"Please sit for a moment, if you can, André. My friend, Mr. Norton, and I need your help."

I told him about the séance, Miss Dunster, and the message. I showed him the notes I had written out. He studied the message for a few moments and, borrowing my pencil, drew lines between the letters to separate them into words.

"Mon dieu," he said, exploding air from his cheeks, "I sink zat you and your friend are in for it. Za spireet sez to search for a lake of gold, *une lac d'or*. Search for it near the peak of snow, eet sez."

XII

Everyone had heard about Gold Lake. There were old Indian legends about a place, far up in the Sierras, where the Feather River began. Spirit Lake, the Yalesumni called it when they spoke of it to Sutter. A place of strong powers that the Indians fiercely protected with their very lives. Gold poured from that lake in chunks the size of walnuts. Did not the Indians themselves fish with golden hooks and hunt with arrows tipped in gold? In 1850, hundreds had scoured the west slope of the Sierras for the lake. One prospector, a gentleman named Stoddard, claimed to have discovered it, though he was set upon by Indians and driven away from its shores. He told his story and led a company of miners to find the lake, but they only succeeded in locating scurvy in a high valley of the Sierras above Nevada City. They found a lake alright, but no gold lining its shores. They nearly threw Stoddard into it. Instead, they left him, sick and wasted, to find his own way back down the mountainside.

"Eet is terrible in those mountains." André shook his head. "Gold will find you hier better than you will find eet zer."

Norton, however, was determined to go.

"These," he stated, his mouth forming itself into a long, hard line, "are my father's wishes."

And then he added, "My French father. My father the king."

★ ★ ★

In the next few days I walked him around town, trying to convince him that it would be better to start over again in the city than to try for his fortune in those mountains. He had no idea how difficult and heartless it could be.

"You know who they say is luckiest in the placers, Norton?" I asked him as we chuffed to the top of California Street the day after Miss Dunster put that bee in his ear. "You know who falls into a hole lined with gold? A drunken sailor or a crazy mule. And you, my dear fellow, are neither."

"What do the folk of the barrooms and the street corners know about it?" Norton responded. "One must have faith about such things. And follow the lights that are offered. Isn't that what your own mother told you to do?"

I could not quarrel with that.

So I urged him to return to Miss Dunster's for another evening with the spirits, which he did, and it only fortified his belief. This time his father repeated his words and beckoned him, and Norton was even more resolved than ever.

I sought confirmation of my uneasiness elsewhere and took Norton to others who were skilled at predictions. There were many in San Francisco in those days who would look into your future and, for a small sum, advise you where to invest or who to marry, or what day of the week to be cautious on. One Chiliana, Maria Concha—Maria Seashells, they called her—was well known for her unfailing accuracy. She unwrapped her cards from the flowered silk kerchief in which she folded them and laid their well-worn faces out slowly for Norton: the cups, the fool, and the hanged man, the sticks, the cups again, the king.

"Things change swiftly for you, sir," she said, studying Norton's face. "You do well one day, a fool next day, beaten down, left to hang upside down, but then you strike it rich again, no? It has not happened yet? No? It will."

"You see," Norton said as we left Maria's shack by the water. "They all say the same thing. When do we begin?"

XIII

Finally, I took Norton back to Abe Warner's.

"Scheiszkopf! Grandfather! Aufspringer! Aaawwwk! Scheiszkopf!"

"Pedro's talking German today," Abe observed good naturedly. "He likes you two, I think."

The old monkey had found his way onto Norton's shoulder, and together they examined the artifacts lining the room while I talked with Abe. I told him about the evening with Miss Dunster that I attended, and the one I did not. I told him about Maria's cards and the phrenologist, Dr. van Hook, a student of the famous Fowlers, who examined Norton's cranium and pronounced that he had never seen such royal hemispheres in his entire professional career.

"Here was a skull," he announced, "destined for great deeds and exceeding good fortune."

He had even made a map of the declivities of Norton's head, with all its seams and orbs, which Norton quite proudly unfolded later that evening, as one might a chart of some fabled land, and displayed it for Abe.

"It's hopeless," I said. "Everything I've tried to do to deter him has only made him more determined than ever to go on this chase. You know what the chances are of him finding this treasure on his own? Look at him. Can you see him up to his waist in river water? Or rocking a Long Tom in the muck?"

"Then you'd better go." Abe was making chowder for the mechanics and fishermen who would fill his place for lunchtime in a few hours.

"What do you mean, *me*?"

"Well, you're not going to let him go alone, are you?"

"But I was nearly murdered the last time I landed in the diggings, and two of my friends were."

"Then you know the ropes, don't ya? He needs someone like you around."

I'd never thought of myself as experienced in that way, but Abe was right, though I could hardly admit it at the time.

"Yes, but he's chasing a chimera," I went on.

"A who?" Abe asked, chopping a whiting into little pieces.

"A phantom, a dream. This dream of his father, the king."

"Oh, I don't know that it's all a phantom."

"You mean, you agree with Miss Dunster and Norton?"

"Well, let me put it to you this way. I see lots of fellers in this place, and I hear lots of stories. And folks have been telling me about bonanzas that they found and then lost since I started scrubbing this bar and stirring this pot. Sometimes it's lost to another miner what comes in later and digs a foot away from where the other's been scratchin' for weeks and strikes it big. Sometimes it's lost to chance and nature.

"I had a feller in here a few months ago. He gave me this." Abe produced a crumpled piece of paper that showed what looked like the fingers of a hand, and above it some scratches, like unfinished teeth, and mixed in among the teeth, three small circles, with an X through one of them.

"It looks like a child's drawing to me, of a hand and a face, maybe," I said, shifting the paper, studying it from various angles.

"Well, there you are. You see some fingers and a face. This feller says it's a map. He says it's to Gold Lake—the one with the X in it, a course—the one everyone's been looking for all these years. He says he found it. Came across it late one evening back in October way up in the mountains. He was at the end of his provisions and starting to think about eating his mule. He had sores on the backs of his legs, that's the scurvy, and the chilblains mixed in as well—it was getting pretty cold up there already. So he reconnoitered the lake the next morning, did a little digging and saw some rich color in the ground, and then hit bedrock and nuggets a foot down. He filled a poke with these and packed up. He could see the storm coming that morning, and got halfway down before it hit, covering him and his mule with ice. The mule slipped on the rocks and went over, and he barely made it himself, hanging on to the side of the mountain all the way down.

"It was a cold rain in the valley, but he set to walking, knew if he stopped he'd be lost for good. He managed some miles before nightfall. Then he collapsed in some bushes by the trail. A gang of Chinese miners found him the next morning. They were staying far away from the American camps where they get beaten up and robbed and slapped with taxes. They spoke little English, but they stopped to help him anyway, gave him a little of what they had and pointed him toward where they thought he'd find some settlers. He stumbled along for days. Then he found a farm. Folks there took care of him good, he said. He told them his story, even offered them the map. But they said they didn't want it. They were happy in the valley and didn't want to turn it into another Sutter's Mill. They asked him not to tell, either, even offered to set him up with a few acres near them, and he could dig there when he wanted. He said he wouldn't, but that he had business in San Francisco—he'd come down here and see if his wife had written him with news of his family. She might already have tried to come west to meet him.

"Well, one evening, in he stumbles, looking like he just crawled out of a vat of rubbish, all patched together and hobbling along like every step was agony. He asked me if he might have something to drink and pushed a few pennies onto the bar. I gave him a toddy, and he started to tell me his story. I gave him a second, and a bowl of chowder, and he finished his tale. He'd come down to San Francisco to collect his mail and found that his wife had thought him lost and gone off with another. The children were hungry and she couldn't manage the farm on her own. So she sold it and moved into town, went through the money from the farm and all the charity she could stand, till a man from the next town, whose wife had died, asked her to come to his place. He was an honest, kind man, and she had no choice, so she did. She'd be on her way west in a flash to meet her dear Thomas, for that was the pospector's name, if he would only write and tell her where to go and send her enough for the journey.

"Well, he'd already gone through most of the gold that he took away from the lake to get to San Francisco, and he went through the rest on drink after he read that letter. It didn't take long, with the kind of stuff they put in the whiskey down along the docks for him to get pretty sick.

"He could not write her back, he told me. I said I could write and would gladly do that for him if he'd like. He said that wasn't it, he knew his letters. He just knew that he couldn't drag her all the way out here now that she had found a place back home. It wouldn't be right to uproot her again. Better for her, better for the children if they stayed put. 'Like the song says, I'm a used-up man,' Tom said. He was standing right where you are when he said it.

"I said, 'Never mind that, Tom. You just stay here for a while. There's a cot in the back room you can sleep on. It ain't much, but it's warm and you can rest up a little and then see what you want to do.'

"So he stayed for three days. I fed him crabs and chowder and got him a new suit of clothes. But you could tell they didn't fit. Nothing fit right anymore. One night he drew this map for me and told me to go and get the gold. 'It's just waiting for you there,' he says. 'You can pick it up with your hands, I'm tellin' you.' And the next morning he was gone. That was six months ago, and he ain't been back since."

"Abe, there are hundreds of stories like this floating around the city all the time. If word of it gets out, there'll be thousands of miners heading up north to find this lake again. How do you know he was telling you the truth?"

"Well, I don't know, not for sure. But your friend Norton there needs to go looking for a lake of gold, and I happen to have a map. Isn't that passing strange? And if it's true, your friend here will get back on his feet, and I'll build a restaurant on the ocean side with my share, with a dock for a little steamer that will take people out from the city for the day. How about it? Even shares."

XIV

And so, on a cool June morning in 1859, I was on a boat with Norton heading up the river to Sacramento and beyond. I did not know what lights I was following. Would I be honoring my mother's spirit and my own? I did not know. I only could say that circumstances had brought me here. We had borrowed everything, which is to say, I had used up my credit, wherever I had it, throughout the city. Of course, I spent my savings, close to a thousand dollars. We bought clothing for the trip, including warm jackets and and other gear, as well as two new Colt revolvers for each of us. I even took pains to teach Norton how to shoot his weapon in the dunes west of the city, on the way to the ocean. He waved his pistol casually, talking while I was readying a target, and pointing it in every direction—at the sky, at the sea oats, at my head. But once he concentrated on the task, he became an astoundingly good shot. He would be comparing the sand hills here with the shore dunes around Cape Town, and how curious it was that he was to find himself in two such cities, then he would shoot three or four bullets at the target without so much as a second to aim, and then return to his conversation without having missed a word. I could tell by the way the paper of the target exploded like confetti in the air, that all the bullets of his .31 had hit the mark.

Mrs. Palmer put up a hundred dollars for her share.

"Of course you must go, if it means that much to him," she told me. "He's a dear, defenseless person, so you must take good care of him. But you'll see. The trip will do you good as well."

Theodore Hightalling added five hundred dollars on the strength of Mrs. Palmer's convictions. We swore them both to secrecy. To my employer, George Fitch, at the *Bulletin*, I told a different tale—about needing to get away from the city for a while, to travel to the far northern parts of the state, to drive the doldrums from my head, and to see a little of the world before I grew too listless to see it properly, on my own two feet. I would visit an old friend who had begun to farm in the far northern part of the valley, and if I could manage the journey, I would continue on to Mount Shasta. He offered me a furlough for the summer and agreed to pay me for articles I would dispatch about these regions, and especially for the most salacious of these that I could discover—tales of banditry and heroism, stalwart accomplishments and curious customs. Anything that might fill a few sticks with tantalizing copy.

"Please, no reports on grain production or the apricot harvest. I've plenty of those. Give me stories to chill the bones and fire the passions."

Much to my surprise, Randolph Johnson—my dour friend on the paper, and the same artist who was there when I found Norton on the Pacific Street Wharf—overheard the conversation and decided to accompany me. He had had enough of town life, too, he declared. It made his lines stale, to be forever drawing pictures of fires and fancy dances in hotel ballrooms, and the endless procession of politicians, and portraits of aging singers and thespians, who visited the city frequently, now that the streets were being paved and they didn't have to step on a cat's cadaver to get into a carriage. He wanted some time in nature, he said, and wherever we were going, he would go as well, and pay his own way. He was stronger than he looked and would hold up his end of the bargain, he said. He would even supply me with pictures to send back to the *Bulletin*, and that way we might both make a little profit on the journey.

"It would be very good indeed," Norton said, when I consulted him about Randolph's desire to join our party, "for there to be someone to record our adventures. For posterity, you know."

"Norton, now I must say this. Please don't speak to anyone about what we want to do or where we are going. If our secret is exposed, there will be many more people traveling this road with us."

I needed to have this conversation with him often, and on several occasions he very nearly confessed our purposes to former acquaintances on the street, whom he eagerly engaged in conversation now, assuring them that he would soon be back in business. They, of course, would ask about his prospects. And once he even answered that his prospects were excellent, for, in fact, there would be gold enough for all where he was going prospecting.

"Tut, tut, my good fellow," said the acquaintance, a man named Sands with furtive eyes and a scraggly beard punctuated with egg yolk and snuff, as he nervously brushed aside Norton's remark with a wave of his agitated hand. "There's only fool's gold left out there now. Better to invest in some solid mining stock. Let the chaps with the capital do the mining."

It was harder for me to persuade Norton not to speak about our plans with Miss Dunster, whom Norton continued to visit, right up to the evening of our departure. They had become close over these weeks, and Norton was able to confide his doubts and worries and the story of his losses to her, and I am sure he would have fallen to his knees and pleaded for her hand in marriage had we stayed in town a day longer. They would sit in the lobby of the hotel, earnestly discussing their deepest hopes, gazing into each other's eyes until discretion, in the form of Miss Dunster's mother, interrupted their colloquies, just as Norton took Miss Dunster's hands in his. Mrs. Dunster could see that Norton offered her daughter little security beyond his undying admiration and his awkward, urgent attentions.

"We will hope to see you on the return from your business travels," Mrs. Dunster said formally to Norton in parting. The Dunsters were themselves leaving in several days to visit Monterey, Sacramento, and several other larger towns in the valley to spread the word about the Other World to those weary of the sadness and uncertainty of this one.

"I will cherish our meeting, Miss Dunster, and will always be your faithful servant," Norton replied, and bowed to her as she was escorted with severe ceremony up to their rooms.

As we returned to the Birches, he revealed to me a heart that she had braided for him from her perfumed hair. He wrapped it in a spotless piece of white cloth and carried it in the pocket over his own heart.

XV

The sidewheels on the *Whippet* churned the greenish water of San Pablo Bay into its wake, and San Francisco disappeared in the mist. I had vowed never to go in search of gold again, and had prided myself on not having chased Mammon mindlessly as most of those who came to the city did. I still dreamed of that night on the North Fork, and I believed there to be a curse on all such enterprises. Let the gold rest in the earth, I often thought, and let us give our attentions to the happiness of our lives, to our families and friends, to the progress of our great democracy, to any worthy cause that called on us. But the pursuit of wealth was not, I believed, one of these.

Everyone thought me eccentric, to say the least, to hold such views in the most gold-addled place on this earth.

Still, here I was. Following my lights. Something within now told me I should not, could not let Norton go alone chasing this dream which I had helped to encourage. Even if every mile of our trip to Sacramento cried out to me that this dream was taking me to a place I did not wish to go. The small settlements that appeared on either side were really little more than a few cabins, most with broken backs, perched along the ravaged riverbanks or sitting forlornly in the neglected fields. Flotsam from eight years of fevered, profligate searching choked the stream with wreckage in spots, before it floated clear and down to the Pacific on the river's swift current. And yet, even amid this sorry effluence, some had set up housekeeping in holes dug into the riverbank, or in arbors spread between the trees. A number of these gaunt souls stood proudly in our view beside their simple homesteads and waved cheerfully to us as we splashed by.

Randolph could not conceive that the Norton next to him was the same desperate man he had seen a few months earlier on a foggy pier. He and Norton quickly became friends. For his part, Norton expressed his admiration for Randolph's gift for rendering a scene expertly with a few deft strokes of his pencil. He drew several sketches of Norton standing in various poses against the railing of the *Whippet*, which pleased the latter enormously.

"We should honor the artist above all others," Norton pronounced. "If I were Emperor, you, sir, would be the most celebrated artist of the day. You would paint all the empire's portraits, ceilings, and frescoes, you could design buildings and parks if you'd like."

"Well, I don't know if I'm up for all that, your highness," Randolph joked. "I thought that I was on holiday."

In San Francisco, Randolph was well known for his sharp features that often seemed pinched, like a preacher who's just smelled out an unsavory sinner, and a mouth that could twist into an arrogant smirk with the most casual remark. But he had already begun to relax noticeably as we traveled further from the city.

"Now, tell me again exactly where it is that we're off to?" Randolph asked me.

"I won't know till we get to Sacramento," I replied.

That was true. We had not let Randolph in on all our our plans, but I did not know some of these plans myself. My old friend Eric from the *Coventry* had written me in his improving English the year before to say that he had become a man of the land. With his earnings from mining, he had bought some property to the west of Red Bluff, a little more than a hundred miles above Sacramento, and was planting grapes, barley, wheat, an orchard, and every kind of vegetable. Life was good for him there, and he urged me to make the journey to visit him some time. I wrote back as soon as I knew that we would be going, and once Abe had explained the mysterious geography of the map to me, it seemed like it would be comfortably on our way. I asked Eric to write to me care of the post office in Sacramento with specific instructions about how to reach his farm. I said I would be bringing a friend with me (I had not counted on Randolph at the time), that I was writing articles for the paper about my travels. But I remained silent about our other plans.

In Sacramento, we had to wait for nearly a week until Eric's letter arrived. We busied ourselves inspecting the levee that had been built to protect the city from its regular flooding; we took long walks in the countryside, and out to Sutter's Fort, which had fallen into complete disrepair, its doors had long since disappeared to make a sluice for a nearby digging. Someone had even helped himself to many of the bricks from the outside wall.

Sutter had retired to Hock Farm, his house on the Feather River, where he licked his wounds and continued to prosecute his suit for redress against the state and the hordes who had pillaged his empire. Most of New Helvetica was gone, carved into a thousand pieces by squatters and politicians and the courts.

Marshall, Sutter's foreman, who had discovered the first kernel of gold that summoned the rest of the world, could not seem to find another. They said he now spent his days in his cabin on the American, soaking in liquor, unable to move himself from the table in front of the window.

Sacramento remained crowded with miners. Many still came west expecting a promised land, and many others resolved to take advantage of them. The old Round Tent with its licentious pictures was gone, replaced by sturdy saloons and gambling halls that would take you for every cent nonetheless. There was an air of prosperity to the place, brought by the Capitol, and the graft and commerce that followed it to town.

We saw mountain men and old forty-niners, mixed in with street preachers and drovers, scores of the latter, since the city had become a center for the overland shipping routes as well as the river traffic.

Even the famous Chinese giant Chang Woo had been engaged to fill a music hall with his eight-foot presence, along with an acrobatic troop. Fifty cents a visit. We attended a dazzling performance by Lotta Crabtree, the twelve-year-old *méchante enfant*, darling of the mining camps, with a cast of twenty-seven other children, in *The Brigand*. That set us each back five dollars. But grizzlies on leads were paraded through town for free, and one that had been trained by a Russian danced mazurkas to the melodies of a banjo played by a little boy.

One saloon proudly exhibited a large glass jar with the pickled head of the famous bandit, Joaquin Murieta, next to the one in which floated the hand of another desperado, Three-Fingered Jack. There had been other heads of Joaquin displayed in the state, and no one was ever sure which one was his, even though the bounty hunters had collected the reward and robberies by the famous bandit had ceased. But there were plenty of others left in the hills to inspire stories of infamy and to provide trophies for the posses that gave them chase—Rattlesnake Dick and Tom Bell, along with others without such famous names, like Jumping Joe and Pete Behind the Bush.

Randolph sketched these scenes, and I wrote a squib called "The Kaleidoscope of Sacramento" and sent it off to Fitch.

Eric's letter arrived within the week. It excitedly explained, in its childlike hand, that we should take a boat as far as Red Bluff and, once there, ask for the road that led to Blossom, and once in Blossom to ask anyone for the directions to German Eric's place, and we were sure to find it. Everyone was waiting to see me again.

"Blossom?" Randolph asked.

"That's what it says," I replied. "Unless it means something else in German."

"Who is 'everyone'?" Norton asked.

"I think it's just a mistaken pronoun," I replied, though it also left me puzzling.

XVI

We booked our passage on an even smaller steamer that could navigate the Sacramento up to Red Bluff, the *Bessie Mae*, with its garrulous skipper, John Rogers, who was not much older than I was when I first arrived in California.

"Now I'm not saying you might not have to get out and push her a little, if the channel's low," he said, laughing through the beard that covered his broad face. "There's so much silt from all the mines washing into the Sacramento that it gets shallower every year. But *Bessie* is a light little thing and doesn't draft much, so we should slide by. What are you bringing on board? Any extra weight?"

"Well, just ourselves and our heavy hopes," Randolph said. Rogers's face lit up with the quick joke.

The hundred miles to Red Bluff took us two days of meandering through the heart of the valley and its rich farm and pasture land, past Sutter Buttes to the east, and then to Colusa, where we tied up on the first night. Since there was just one hotel in the town, and that one full, we spent the night on the *Bessie Mae*, curled up in bedrolls that Rogers provided for us.

Norton was intrigued by the expanses to either side of us and murmured something about it being a beautiful place for an empire, especially now that the rolling hills were golden in the morning sun.

"Your spirits seem to have truly lifted, Norton," I said to him one day.

"You know, we don't have to go through with this now. Just say the word and we can call this a splendid holiday and return after a visit with Eric."

"Indeed, not," he said, awaking from his reverie. "How can I disobey my father's wishes? Would you have me do that?"

★ ★ ★

Randolph drew incessantly—quick, thumbnail sketches in a small tablet no bigger than an inch square—in which he rendered astounding likenesses of the landscape and the activity aboard the ship—the deckhands at their work, Captain Rogers with his hat pushed back on his head.

We reached Red Bluff late on the second day and tied up at its single wharf. It was a lively little river town, with the usual scramble of saloons and boarding houses, for the miners pushing off for the mountains to the west, all the way to Eureka on the coast. There had been no big strikes yet, not like those on the American, but there was enough to tantalize people along the Trinity River in among the folds of the Coastals.

We stayed in town that night, at a damp, dirty hotel that charged us ten dollars each for the privilege of lying on a slab of wood and wrapping ourselves in blankets that others had been sleeping in just a few hours before, and washing ourselves with leftover bath water.

Before going to bed, we went to the Empire House saloon next door for a glass of beer, and there, on the bar, next to the pigs feet, sat another large glass jar, with a head floating in its pickling brine, and a sign nearby that read, "The Head of Joaquin Murieta." The sign was old and splattered with food and drink, the head was hideously distorted, the hair moved like water weeds if you poked the side of the jar with an elbow, as I mistakenly did.

"He must have had two heads," Randolph reasoned.

Norton refused to go near this horror.

In the morning, the manager of the hotel, Mr. Mercer, spoke with us about death over our breakfast of eggs and bacon.

"Have you ever considered," he mused, cleaning the wax from his ear, "what will happen to you after the Grim Reaper has cut you down?"

"Why no," Randolph replied, "I hadn't thought about that yet this morning."

"Well, you may scoff," Mercer continued, "but I think of it often."

"And . . . ?" Randolph goaded him on.

"And I think I would simply like to be left in an open field once I'm gone. Let nature take its course. The animals can have whatever they want, and the rest will turn into fertilizer. No fuss."

Randolph nodded. "Pleasant thought. Goes well with the biscuits."

After we had explored the subject more through our second cups of coffee, he consented to change the topic when I asked if he could give us instructions for Blossom.

"Just follow the track going west from town a few miles and yer there. Can't miss it, though there's nothin' much there."

I inquired about Eric.

"Sure, German Eric. He's a good sort. A little slow, if you get my drift. But a good sort. Haven't seen him much lately. Must be pretty busy. Tell him Walter at the Garden House says hey."

We set off along the rutted path for Blossom, with our luggage strapped to our backs, dipping up and over and down the rolling hills. Within an hour we came upon a cabin, in a clearing to the right, made from logs, with a high peaked roof and a second story. Next to the house was an arbor, with benches under the trees. Behind the house was a barn and beyond that fields of wheat and corn. A small grove of fruit trees, all in flower, and grape vines filled several of the hillsides, and in the distance, I could see a tall, lanky shape tending the vines. Eric. A large, black dog barked up to us and then held his ground between us and the house, eyeing us carefully. We waited. I could see Eric beginning to move toward us, but before he had cut the distance in half, a young woman appeared from the house.

Beneath her flowered head scarf, blue eyes glistened from her smooth, tanned face. She smiled at us politely and called the dog away.

"Come, Chorninka, come to me. They are friends." Then she looked at us and laughed, despite herself, and added, "I think."

I began to introduce ourselves, but within moments, Eric was there embracing me and then shaking hands with Norton and Randolph. It had been a long time and much had happened, and it began to spill out as he wiped away his tears and showed us to the arbor. Irina, his wife, brought us trays of food and drink, fresh dark bread and butter, slices of rich meat, pickled tomatoes and fruits, glasses of fiery vodka—in a bottle with peppers and dill.

We drank and feasted and Eric told his story.

★ ★ ★

He had stayed with Nikolai and the others after I had gone back to San Francisco, and they had continued prospecting, to moderate success. Several of the group had even gone back up the river to the sad spot that we had worked, but it had already been claimed by others and the banks scoured clean of gold. They had panned a little from the leavings, but it barely paid their expenses for the two weeks of labor. Besides, Nikolai wanted to move on to a different place after the unhappiness that had beset us all on the North Fork. They changed their camp to the Feather River, where they followed the same plan, settling on a spot near Pulga and then branching out to try other diggings. But it was already crowded. Nikolai often visited old man Sutter at his ranch. They had known each other before the Rush and had remained friends. He urged Nikolai to get some land before the rascals had grabbed it all. They weren't honoring his deeds with the Mexican government from before the war, but he still had friends, and he knew of several parcels that would be right for any kind of farming one could wish. A good investment, because the gold was going to run out. On the east slope of the Coastals, which protected them. Good strong afternoon sun. Plenty of water and timber nearby.

"So vee kom out here und meet up mit other Russians," he continued. "Irina ist Nikolai's cousina, und vee figgur out da rest.

"Nikolai lives close, und many of the group you vill remember also. They haf farms too. Nikolai calls his a dacha. Is avay from all da peeples in da Sierras, but is still vild enuf for da Russians. Serdu is here alzo. He hunts und traps in da mountains, und every six monaten he kom here, to us, stay a couple days, und den is gone. Und mostly Steven go mit him."

"And how is Steven?"

"Did I not tell you? He just lives over da hill, over der. He has a small place, but he likes it dat way. Did you not hear about his accident? He loos his hand in da mountains. It vas frostbite. He vas all alein in da hills. Vent to seek his vision, he ses, und vas ketched in early snowstorm. He vas trapped for beinah two weeks, und ven he got down from da mountain, he hand vas black und *wheeu!* did it stink. But you vould never know he's mitout one. He vorks his place by himself und he disappears mit Serdu sometimes und dey get lost in da mountains—they know dem all, from da Trinity Alps to Shasta und over to da Varners und back down to da Crystals. Dey go every place."

"Then I must speak to them," I said, and explained our purposes, showing him the map. Randolph was surprised, since it was the first time he knew anything about our other destination.

"Yes, vee vill go over der dis afternoon."

"Were you going to tell me? Or just slip away some night?" Randolph said later. He was clearly hurt. "You could have trusted me, you know."

"I know that now," I said.

We saw Steven for more feasting and I talked to him about his accident, which he waved away without a moment's self-indulgence. And then we studied the map.

"Yes, I think I know where this is. I know the five fingers of these rivers well. The best way up is along the Sacramento, the first finger after the thumb. That's really just a creek, Backbone Creek. I've been to Shasta once, but not beyond, not this way. This is beyond," he said excitedly. "It's two weeks, maybe three. Depending on how fast we move. When do we start?"

XVII

We talked late into the night about outfits and gear, the best routes to go to attract the least attention. The last thing that we wanted was to start a rush of any kind.

"Let's wait a little for Serdu," Steven advised. "I'd like to take him with us. He knows things that no one else does about these mountains."

So we waited, and in the meantime, we visited Nikolai at his dacha several miles away, which he called "The Beautiful Place." And it was. He had built a frame house with verandas all around it, places to watch the world go by in the evening. His children were growing, and there was activity everywhere, games and songs, and time for long evenings around a table they set up under the trees.

"You've come back," he said. "This is good. We were beginning to think that we would never see you again.

You know how people get lost out here. Tell me, why do you go in search of gold again?"

I tried to explain, but I could see he was not sympathetic.

"For what? My friend, let me find you all some land near us, and you can farm it. Norton, here, can be king of his own castle. And our artist, Mr. Randolph, can have a place to draw right here if he wishes. Why are you chasing after these dreams?"

"Because, my dear sir," Norton answered, "there are some dreams that you must follow. You of all people can appreciate that. Look at what you have here—a beautiful family, a lovely piece of land, comfort and joy. But for some of us, who have lost everything, who can not hold our heads high when we go to town, who have not found that beautiful place, we need to search a little longer."

Nikolai nodded and drank his tea in silence.

"You know, in my country," Norton continued, "they tell a story about a bird. It has a funny name, the Oof Bird. It's about a poor young man who lived alone outside a village and scratched out a living on the small farm that his parents had left to him after they died. It was such a meager piece of land that he could raise little. None encouraged him to court their daughters, so he toiled on by himself.

"In the forest nearby, everyone said, there lived a bird that was beautiful beyond belief. But no one had ever seen the bird, it was so quick that it flew away before anyone could get close enough to catch even a glimpse of its feathers. But everyone had heard the bird's song that filtered through the trees of the forest. In the evenings they sat at their windows and listened while it sang:

"My eggs are made of shining gold,
But who shall find them must be pure
Bitter wind and rain endure
Or he will search till he grows old.

"Everyone thought the song was quite lovely, and everyone in the village wondered, where *does* that bird lay its eggs? Many looked high and low for the bird's nest, and many simply dreamed of finding its golden eggs. Finally, everyone forgot about looking for them and told their children that the eggs were only a legend and did not really exist at all.

"But the young man heard the song and decided that he would find the eggs. He did what no one else had done before. He followed the sound of the bird, even though he could not see it. It was not an easy journey. He had to climb steep mountains and ford raging rivers, and always the bird was just ahead of him. But he never stopped, except to sleep a little or to eat a few berries, and he followed that bird's song until he could go no farther. He was in the deepest part of the forest. All was dark, he had lost his way, and he was now without food or water. He commended himself to his Maker, and fell asleep, thinking he might never awaken again. When he did, though, a bird was sitting on a low branch of a tree near him, and it sang:

*"Just one more day, stay strong and true,
The golden eggs will wait for you.*

"He could barely crawl through the trees, but he did till evening when he collapsed and drifted off again into exhausted sleep.

"When he awoke this time, he found that a bird was lying dead on the ground before him. He was so hungry that he thought about eating the bird for breakfast, but instead, he took pity on it and scratched a hole in the earth and laid the bird to rest beneath the leaves.

"When he did this, the bird he had been following began to sing its beautiful song again, very close to where the young man lay. He struggled to his feet and followed the bird's song again and, this time, he had only gone a little way when the forest opened up and there, in the midst of the clearing, sat the Oof Bird on a nest of eggs made of rare gold. The bird looked quite ordinary. In fact, it looked exactly like the bird that had fallen from the sky and that the young man had buried that morning.

"'You have shown bravery and perseverance and, most important, you have shown compassion, and that is why I give these eggs to you.'" And with that, the bird spread its wings and offered the young man the contents of its nest.

"He thought, 'I cannot take everything, and leave nothing for the bird or another who searches.' And so, in the end, he took only one egg and a few pieces of straw from the nest.

"'Ah,' said the bird, 'that is a good choice.'

"And with that it invited the young man to climb on its back and swiftly returned him to his village, much to the astonishment of all.

"But once the novelty of his accomplishment had worn off, people began to laugh at him. 'You took only one? What a fool!' his neighbors said.

"Still, the young man knew what he needed. When he sold the egg, he used the money well. And once that egg was gone, another took its place on the little nest of straw in the morning. All his endeavors were blessed, and soon he married a kind and lovely woman. Together they prospered and were happy, and he never failed to thank the bird each day for its gift."

There was quiet on the porch.

"You see, I don't want all the eggs," Norton said to Nikolai. "I just want one. And one for each who follows the Oof Bird's song with me."

XVIII

Serdu arrived two days later, looking older, grizzled, his face lined like an ancient chart, but with the same spring to his steps. He was carrying a huge pack—he had just walked over the mountains from the coast—but it seemed weightless on his back.

"Cap-i-tain!" he called to me and saluted.

He knew where we wished to go. And he knew the little lake. He had not prospected there, but he had stayed there on its shores one night.

"Lake talkin'," he said, "talkin' all time. Say 'You go way. No stay!' Her magic lake."

We sat around the table and planned the trip. We bought horses and mules in Red Bluff, at separate times and from different dealers. We did the same with our other gear, our bedding, tools, and provisions. As far as the town was concerned, there were a few new prospectors around—nothing unusual, especially for some greenhorns from San Francisco to want to try their luck.

Only John Rogers and Walter Mercer could have put the three of us together. Rogers was back down the river and we carefully avoided meeting Mercer.

It was the second of July before we could leave, a little late to be going, but Serdu thought we should make good time. He preferred to walk, and once we had loaded his pack onto a mule, he moved as quickly as any of us on horseback.

We took the long way around Red Bluff, following a meandering creek to Cottonwood and then up past Anderson and Redding, through little Shasta and then along the river up into the hills. It was rugged, forlorn country, with high canyon walls, but the banks of the river were wide enough to take us all the way up. The mountain grew larger at the mouth of the river, its snowy peak hovering ahead of us between the steep valley walls. We could not come this way in the springtime, when the river would be twice its size, and even now we had to be careful about where we camped: if a rainstorm hit at that time of year, we might suddenly find our selves floating back to Sacramento. But Serdu was cautious, knew what a good place was, and kept us moving until we found one.

Norton and Randolph needed time getting used to their saddles and the rigors of the road, but within a week, they had stopped groaning every time they hauled themselves on or off their horses. The animals were fresh, the weather fine, and so we had a grand time. Randolph drew the Sacramento canyon, and I described it in my journal, but we sent nothing to Fitch about this.

We camped in the foothills of Mount Shasta on July 14, and Serdu performed a purifying rite at the base of the mountain the next morning. Steven went with him to offer prayers with the smoke of sweet grasses, which Serdu bundled together and lit before the mountain. He returned an hour later with the smoking sticks and waved them over each of us, passing the smoke around our bodies.

"This make clean," he said. "Is good."

"Are you some kind of Indian?" Randolph asked. "Aren't you from Siberia?"

"Is same. Same peoples. Come here on ice, many many years gone," Serdu told him.

"Must have been the first Gold Rush," Randolph kidded him.

"No," Serdu said. "Caribou. Caribou Rush, my people say."

XIX

At night, with the full moon, Mount Shasta gave off a soft silver light that illuminated our camp site. Norton sat up late that night, gazing at it. But we skirted the mountain itself and picked our way over the hills that issued from it like the roots of a colossal tree made of rock and snow. It is an awesome presence. No wonder the Indians of that land held it sacred and believed it the home of the Great Spirit.

Indeed, we were taking a great risk traveling this close to the mountain. Fearing that we might anger the Indians of that place, the Shastas, despite the gifts that he had insisted we bring with us to purchase our safe passage through their lands, Serdu hurried us along, first south and then north and east around its slopes. We could already see another mountain in the distance, half as high as Shasta.

"We go," Serdu pointed to it. And by sundown we were within its shadow, sheltered between the valley made by two ridges that descended from its summit. "Tomorrow we go up. The lake she talkin'." Serdu pointed to the top of the mountain.

The next day we climbed through the chilly morning. We left the horses and mules down below in the camp, with Randolph and Steven, while Serdu, Norton, and I clambered to the summit with provisions for a new camp on the lake. It took us till early that afternoon, following Serdu's swift lead up the mountainside, sometimes leaping with a full pack over dangerous fissures, scrambling over gravel that gave way as quickly as he found new footing, but never slowing down. It was all Norton and I could do to keep up with him, and even then we didn't. He was easily a quarter mile ahead of us by the time we reached the lip of the summit and pulled ourselves over into that spectacular valley, with its glistening blue lake. The lake was perhaps a mile in length and half that in width.

"Well, Norton, here it is. Your father's lake of gold."

And in the light from the setting sun, it was truly so.

We made camp and, as he had before, Serdu again went through a similar rite by the side of the lake, waving smoking wands of sweet grass into the evening air, bowing to the lake, murmuring aloud to it, asking for its forgiveness for the desecration we were about to commit.

We all slept restlessly. The wind sang in the rocks. I heard the cries of my lost friends, the sounds of the crashing sea, the storms of my childhood dreams. I do not know what Norton or Serdu heard, but I doubt any of us slept much that night.

The next day we searched the shore. There seemed to be no stream running out of the lake as Willie told Abe, which made me doubt the truth of the story. Gold was not lying on the shore for us to scoop up into our sacks. In fact, it looked like a very unpromising place for us to be looking at all. And if this was the source of the gold in the valley, that fact hid itself well.

Serdu let us search, while he contemplated the surface of the lake. I showed Norton how to pan, dipping water from the lake to swirl through the dirt I'd dug from its bank. We worked our way around the lake, testing for color every hundred yards or so. But we came up wet and dirty and without even a fleck of gold for our day's labor.

"I don't know about this place," I muttered over our fire that evening. It was already beginning to get cold at that altitude, even in the middle of summer. "Let's give it another day or two and then move on. Maybe there's another place that fits this map."

"No," Norton said. "There's something here. But it's not going to tell us its secrets right away."

I had heard about his father's command more times than I could remember, and so I asked him to tell me about growing up in the south of Africa, and he warmed to the idea.

"It was odd. We were settlers. The government gave us a piece of land on the Fish River, a desolate place, that my father tried to farm. I would stare across the river at the young men from the tribes on the other side. They came to watch as we built our cabin. They wore a strip of cloth around their middles and carried long spears. They could easily have swum across the river and killed us all, but they never did, and we never ventured across to their side. Strange that people should live this way, so separate from each other. I remember wondering what it might be like to be a young warrior, and there was a time when I longed to join them, anything but do another day's chores on the farm and watch these people I called my parents use up their strength in that hard ground. It seemed to me the most futile of gestures. We stayed there for several years until my father—my stepfather—managed to borrow enough money from the other Jews who had been banished to this forsaken corner of the globe to open a store, a trading post really, much like those throughout this valley. I know he did not wish to admit the land had defeated him, but it had. We were all much happier in the store, and in the town, and the work of the store came quickly to him. He had an ease with people that made them trust him. I used to despise this in him and thought it was a great weakness of his. But, in truth, I envy it and wish I had it myself. Instead, what am I but this worthless creature no one has any faith in at all."

I tried to assure him that people trusted him, too. Weren't we all on this expedition as a sign of that confidence? But this did not placate him.

★ ★ ★

Serdu patiently watched over us for two days, as we circled and pecked around the edges of that beautiful lake. We could see that none of the shoreline was disturbed from previous digging. It was pristine and smooth, as though no one had ever walked here before—or if they had, all trace of their footsteps had vanished. Serdu barely moved from the spot he had taken on a large rock that was set into the shoreline, where he listened to the lake's singing. He ate nothing during this time.

On the morning of the third day he began to chant, a slow, steady stream of words that he kept intoning throughout the day. They were not unlike the glassy surface of the lake. In the evening he mixed some powdered herbs from a pouch he carried with him into a gourd of water, and within a few minutes, he had fallen onto his back and began speaking in his mother tongue, we thought, or in some other language that we could not comprehend. For several hours the words surged from him, stopping suddenly, then continuing in a torrent, then slowly dying down to a trickle.

"What has he done to himself?" Norton asked Steven, who had joined us for the day while Randolph sketched in the valley.

"I believe it is an herb that the Indians here take, *tolache* they call it, something from jimson weed. I have seen Standing Black Bear, the holy man of the Wintun, who live around Blossom, drink a potion like this."

"What in heaven's name for?" Norton continued.

"To see things more clearly. For visions."

"What things?"

"Why someone is sick, what spirits are out there to help or harm the tribe, what's in the future."

Still, we were frightened for Serdu, since we did not know what this herb contained, nor what we should do if it went ill with him. And to judge by the declarations of his speech, he was having concourse with beings that we could not see or hear.

In the end he slept, a deep, deathlike sleep of such stillness that I went to check on his breathing several times in the night.

Serdu roused us with the first light.

"Come, come you," he instructed us.

Without waiting for us to pull on our boots, he led us along the shore of the lake, picking his way among the branches of the trees and the bushes that ringed the edge. He was searching for something, and several times he dropped to his knees and put his ear to the earth.

"Here, dig," Serdu said, after almost an hour of testing spots, and marked the place with a large circle that he drew on the ground.

Later that day we found gold several feet down.

They were splashes of gold, each only a few inches in length, with irregular edges but smooth to the touch. It seemed as though they had been spewed, molten, from some furnace within the earth and left in small puddles on the cool rock, like ice that hardens on a cup of water and that you can lift off as it melts away from the sides, a thin membrane, before it becomes watery lace and slips between your fingers. Leaves of gold. Nearly five pounds' worth.

Norton expanded his digging further from the lake and Serdu's circle. We dug as deep as we could. Our shovels sparked against the rock, but we found nothing more.

"That all," Serdu told Norton, smiling. "One eggs."

★ ★ ★

Serdu set us to work around the shore of the lake, smoothing out the places we had disturbed. And then he lit another a bundle of grass and stayed behind to wave the smoke over our departure.

Around the fire that night in the camp below the lake, our company debated whether we should continue the dig.

"Well, you did say that you only wanted one egg," Randolph observed to Norton. "It seems like that is what Serdu's vision has managed to lay."

Norton poked at the ground with a stick.

"Cheer up, Norton," Randolph added. "It could have been a rotten egg. Besides, I have a feeling that something good will come of this, scrambled as it may appear to be now."

"I'm for moving on," Steven said. "And as for my share, I hereby bequeath my portion of the egg to Norton. May it bring him the kingdom he is looking for."

"I'll second that," Randolph replied.

The firelight revealed the emotion that had swept over Norton's face.

"I suppose we should be satisfied," Randolph philosophized. But still we weren't and we all knew it. Maybe one of our mules will stumble into a strike, I thought. But that isn't what happened. The wind blew us another kind of bird.

XXI

Serdu took us back a different way, through the country of the Achomawi, a peaceful people who would happily let us cross their lands in exchange for some of the beads, colored cloth, and small glass bottles we had brought with us for this purpose. Serdu did not want to take the chance of sudden encounters with the Achomawi or any others any longer, and said we had been charmed not to have had a meeting before this time. So that we might sooner meet the Achomawi and make these arrangements, Serdu had us camp in a large clearing near Indian Spring Mountain and light a fire with damp wood so that they would be sure to see our smoke.

Serdu was the first to notice the spot in the southern sky. It grew larger as we followed his finger to the point he indicated above the trees and, with him, we watched the arrival of this unexpected visitor.

"Serdu, did you pour *tolache* in the coffee?" Randolph asked, as the shape drew closer to us, making a sound like churning, beating wings as it approached. We were all too dumbfounded to move.

Within a few minutes it was hovering at the height of the treetops near the long plume of smoke from our fire. The ship of the air was shaped like a long yellow squash over a hundred feet in length. It was ribbed like a boat, with wires secured to these supports from which was suspended a long large box, very much like a small railroad car, with windows on both sides. One of these windows had opened and from it a head appeared and bellowed down at us, "Is this California?"

We exclaimed that it was, and suddenly a rope emerged from the window and was dropped to us.

"Pull me down!" the voice commanded.

And so we did, until the car was only a few feet off the ground. You could tell now that this balloon, for that is what it was, was completely sealed and seemed to be made from a canvas that was coated with a shellac or lacquer the color of honey. Inside the neatly built compartment were benches and a kind of stove—its smoke was funneled through a long pipe that ran out of the car and sent its hot air coursing over a paddle wheel, which in turn made the beating sound we had heard and propelled the craft. Behind this spinning wheel was a rudder for steering, which could be accomplished with a lever mounted at the rear of the cabin.

A lively man, gray at the temples but with an energetic air, leaped from the car. "Rufus Porter," he announced, shaking hands all around, "glad to meetcha."

Grasping the lapels of his jacket and assuming the posture of the orator, Norton declaimed:

> *"There's a fount about to stream,*
> *There's a light about to beam,*
> *There's a warmth about to glow,*
> *There's a flower about to blow;*
> *There's a midnight blackness changing*
>   *Into gray.*
> *Men of thought, and men of action,*
>   *Clear the way!"*

"Ah, sir, you do me such honor," Porter replied.

Norton began the next verse, "Once the welcome light has broken, Who can say..."

Porter picked up the rhyme, "What the unimagined glories of the day."

And together they finished their recitation:

> *"What the evil that shall perish*
>   *In its ray!*
> *Aid the dawning, tongue and pen;*
> *Aid it, hopes of honest men;*
> *Aid it, paper—aid it type—*
> *Aid it, for the hour is ripe,*
> *And our earnest must not slacken*
>   *Into play.*
> *Men of thought, and men of action!*
>   *Clear the way!"*

"Obviously, you know who I am."

"Of course," Norton replied. "I am a devoted reader of your journal, and I've followed your inventions with some interest over the years. I have studied your 'Aerial Navigation,' but never dreamed that I would see your machine in operation."

Before we knew it Norton and Porter were engaged in an arcane discussion of the points of the airship, which he had christened the *Aeriel*, its name embossed in flowing letters on the side of the cabin. Bits of the conversation floated down to us mere mortals.

"The varnish was the tricky part. The first one that I tried ate through the canvas. The second skin was shredded by the local boys. You know, they thought I was a sorcerer. If only those young ignoramuses knew it's just simple mechanics."

"And how is it propelled?" Norton asked.

"Well, I started with wood, but that's pretty heavy to fly on. Then one day I was sitting in the privy. I lit my pipe and threw the match down the hole and the whole thing exploded. Burned my arse and nearly took my manhood. But I knew then my source of fuel."

"Are you telling us that this contraption runs on shit?" Randolph ejaculated.

"Well, you might say so, young fellow," Porter replied quite excitedly. "But it'll also fly on old fruits and vegetables once they start to rot and give off enough gas. And whiskey too, in a pinch. The whole thing could travel quite a distance on a few barrels of whiskey if it's strong enough."

We talked away the rest of the day, and through the evening. We peppered him with questions, and he answered eagerly. He had flown from Maryland to our camp in little more than a week—twice as long as he had promised the world he would require for this part of the journey. But no matter, the time could be trimmed. A southern wind had blown him off course, for he had planned to land in San Francisco. Now that would have caused a sensation and finally, after many years, brought him enough funding from investors to build larger, stronger, faster ships. Aerial locomotives, he had dubbed them. This was his only ship, and he had told no one he was going. In fact, he had kept the construction of the ship a secret until he was certain it could meet his expectations.

"Won't people be missing you?" Randolph asked him.

"Oh, no." Porter swept the question away. "I often go walking for a week or two to see what is happening in the world. No one will think it odd at all that I'm not in my bed for a month. Most especially Eunice—my wife," he nearly whispered her name.

"Why I remember the time I walked from Portland down to New Haven and started a dancing school there for the young ladies. I left one day and was gone for a year. Didn't know if I'd ever make it back down Maine again—but that's another story!" he said with a wink.

XXII

When we awoke we were surrounded by Indians who had followed the airship to the clearing and now had set up their camp in a circle around us. They brought abundant food to prepare a feast, for they thought Porter could be no other than the Great Spirit himself, in one of his many guises. They presented him with gifts—a beautifully wrought headdress, a vest of porcupine quills, and a red stone pipe filled with acrid tobacco which they smoked with him. Serdu translated through signs and the few words that he knew in their own and other native tongues, while Porter talked nonstop with their chief and a priestess of the tribe, a sturdy woman who had tattooed the wings of eagles onto her broad cheeks. Indeed, they sought to give her to Porter in marriage, and Serdu explained, so as not to insult their offer, that the Great Spirit would come back some day for her, once he had completed his travels.

"They want me to stay," Porter told us. "They think

that it's a miracle. I wonder if they'll still think so when they see these machines every week. I hope they don't try to shoot them down."

"I wouldn't worry about the Indians," Randolph chimed in. "It's the miners you'll need to be careful of, especially if they've gotten some bad whiskey. Or if they've been up in the mountains too long, they might think you're something they can eat."

★ ★ ★

Between his colloquies with the Achomawi, Porter busied himself by collecting anything that might burn, as well as all the animal and human droppings about the encampment, to refill his gas container.

"It'll take a few days to begin emitting enough gas, but with the good west wind that's blowing, there shouldn't be a problem with fuel. We can coast home."

The Indians were at first very surprised and then made not a little uneasy by Porter's gathering up the manure of the camp. Eagle Wings was particularly upset about it, and gave an angry speech to all. "He steals shit, he steals inside me," Serdu translated for us.

It was a tenuous moment. They could easily have overpowered us, despite our arms. Serdu was aware of the danger and he told her something in her language loud enough for all to hear.

"What did you say?" I asked him

"Say, shit great gift. Shit make him fly. Shit make him family."

XXIII

While Porter was waiting for his gas to cure, he took Serdu and several of the Indians on a long walk of several days to Mount Shasta, a sight he very much wished to see. At first, the Achomawis were hesitant to go with him, since this took them into their neighbor's lands, and they had not made the polite requests for permission. But if they asked for this, they reasoned they would have to share Porter with the Shastas, and this they did not wish to do. In the end, they simply went. After all, what could go wrong? Were they not in the company of the Great Spirit?

Though he had passed his sixtieth year, Porter set a blistering pace.

"I've been cooped up in that machine too long," he told Serdu.

"Like Serdu you walking," his companion replied, adding to the end of his sentence his highest compliment, "Brother."

After the feasting and excursions, Porter finally loaded his machine with the Achomawis' gifts, all the provisions we could spare, and Serdu, who had decided on their long walk to accept Porter's invitation and accompany him back East.

"He'll be my witness," Porter declared. "I'll bring him back to San Francisco in a few months."

Serdu explained to the Achomawis that he was going with the Great Spirit because he knew so many of the lands they would travel through so well and could translate for him should the need arise. Plainly, they were disappointed, but the chief and Eagle Wings nodded their consent.

With much fanfare, Porter started his boiler and bade us all farewell. We cast off the rope and the ship slowly rose in the air, while the assembled Achumawis raised their hands to him, their gesture of the reverence with which he was held. We all watched for a long time as the ship gathered height above the trees and Porter swung its rudder to catch the west wind and ride the zephyrs back to Bethesda.

★ ★ ★

We later learned that they never made it. Everything went well over the Sierras and the Rockies, and they covered the Great Plains in a day, passing above the astonished, uplifted faces of several wagon trains. They were moving too fast to stop, and so they continued their ride to the east. In the midst of a sudden lightning storm in Ohio, the *Aeriel* crashed in flames. Everything was lost in the fire that swept the machine when it hit the ground. Serdu and Porter barely escaped the conflagration with their lives. They limped to the nearest town and eventually found their way to Washington, where Porter introduced Serdu as a Siberian Indian brought back by air from California.

"That sure is a lot of hot air you're sailing on, Professor Porter," one wag at the *Scientific American* offices needled him. That was all it took for the joke to get around town. "Guess what? Porter is claiming he's flown to California and back in under two weeks, and he's dragged along an old Indian who knows some Russian for proof. The aged one is obviously losing some of his own ballast." Instead of solving his financial worries the disaster that ended their trip made it impossible for Porter to raise a nickel to build another airship, let alone a fleet, though he tried for the next ten years of his life to do so, writing and speaking and sending models of his airships sailing around auditoria up and down the East Coast.

Serdu and Porter soon retired to New England, where they walked the hills together until Serdu told him one day, "Me go back." Porter gave him enough money for a ticket to Saint Louis. The railroad made him ride in the baggage car. Serdu barely escaped Saint Louis alive. Packs of boys hounded him, pelting him with sticks and rocks, dogs were set on him, shots fired in his direction. Serdu kept his head down and walked. The rest of the way. He turned up at Eric's farm one day nearly a year later. It was late spring and the clover was blooming. He was gaunt and barefoot, his clothing in shreds. He slept for a week, Eric's letter read, and rarely went walking very far after that.

"Just to Red Bluff und back," he wrote, "und sometimes to visit his Wintun friends on the Cottonwood for their fests or to go hunting sometimes mit Nikolai. He say he ist getting fat und lazy, but he look so thin, und we feed him lots of butter und cream always. 'One day,' he say, 'I will walk far. Do not comen look for me, and sad be not. I go home and happy be.' "

A year later another letter came from Eric to say Serdu had disappeared during the winter. Eric followed his tracks into the woods until they vanished in the snow. Serdu did not come back with the spring. But sometimes Eric and Irina hear his flute sighing with the trees.

XXIV

What became of us? We had instructions from Serdu on how to find our way back, and Steven knew some of the way as well. We traveled south until we reached the Pit River, and then determined to follow it, with a shortcut below Chalk Mountain to Roaring Creek, to save us the big bend of the Pit and bring us down to the valley.

It was a sound plan, and we made good time, until one morning I saw Steven and Randolph, who were riding together, disappear into the ground in front of me.

The events occurred so quickly that neither Norton nor I could remember all of them distinctly afterwards, much as we tormented ourselves that we might have failed to see the signs of the coming disaster and thus been able to avert it.

The Indians along the Pit, the Ilmawi, I later learned, dug large holes on well-traveled trails to trap their game, a habit that had given the river its name. They covered these pits with brush and leaves and waited for a deer to bound, innocently, into one of their snares. They dug their trenches deep, so the animals could not escape. One of these had consumed our companions.

We spurred our horses to the lip of the chasm into which our friends had fallen, and dismounted. Inside the pit swirled a chaos of shouts and moans, and the cries of the horses, writhing in agony, and, beneath them, Steven and Randolph. Steven was trying to pull free from his saddle, but his right leg was pinned under his horse, which was trying to right itself on the bodies of Randolph and his mount. Its foreleg was broken, and each time the creature set it down the injury sent it into spasms of pain. Beneath his groaning horse, we could see Randolph's shoulders and head at the bottom of the pit, his face twisted up to us, his eyes turned and staring into ours, unblinking, while his horse thrashed on top of him, neighing piteously.

I threw a rope to Steven. He wrapped it around his good arm and together Norton and I pulled him from the sickening darkness of the pit. His leg was broken above the knee and pieces of bone stuck through his trousers. We staunched the bleeding as best we could and propped him up against a tree by the side of the trail so that he did not choke on his vomit. His face was ashen, but he managed to open his eyes and look at his leg and then at us and say, "What a mess I am. Oh, Sweet Lord."

Norton tried to quiet him, to keep him still. He braced his shoulders and gave him soothing words and whiskey, which he had frantically pried from the pack of one of the mules.

The horses still groaned in the pit. I drew my revolver from my jacket pocket and shot each in the forehead. They sighed, deep huffs of breath, and died. Through the blue smoke, I could still see Randolph's eyes. They would not, could not move again.

As we began to attend to Steven's injuries, we were deaf to the sound of horses approaching us on the trail, until they were upon us. Four men who had drawn up their neck scarves to cover their faces, like riders do when the trail is thick with dust.

"So, you have found our surprise," one of them, with bulging eyes declared to us. "Those Diggers' pits catch all sorts of game."

"We need help!" Norton implored.

"Well, that's not in our line," the bug-eyed one replied. "Easy now, leave your pistols be. We'll just relieve you of your gold and your animals and let you to lick your wounds. And that one," he said, pointing to me, "can cook something up for you."

"Were you born without a heart?" Norton cried.

"Who needs one?" Strangely, he was enjoying the conversation. "Do you think anything is going to matter in half an hour to your friend there?" he asked, waving the pistol he had taken from his belt at Steven.

"Let's cut the jawing," one of his confederates interrupted, his hand on the grip of his Colt. "Just give us your gold and we'll be on our way."

Before Norton could answer again, Steven had his pistol in his hand, had cocked it, and shot at the bandits. One fell immediately, mortally wounded in the neck. The others drew their weapons and commenced firing at Steven, sending bullets into his head, his chest, the tree against which he leaned. In the smoke and confusion, Norton freed his own revolvers from his pockets and quickly fired at the other outlaws. Two more tumbled from their saddles, and I added my own bullets to the melee.

Meanwhile their leader wheeled and reared his horse in order to fire at us sideways over the neck of his mount. But before he could get off a shot, Norton sent several bullets in his direction. One tore through his nose and into the front of his face. He bellowed in pain and ripped away the bandana. I could see then what I already knew from his eyes and his remark about me. It was Nast from the *Coventry*.

"You've shot me in the eye, you stinking son a whore!" he shouted, through the bloody pulp that had been his nose and cheek, spitting blood and bone at us. "Goddamn, you've finished me!"

Terrified by the carnage, his horse bolted and took him, holding on to its neck, screaming, back up the path that we had just come down.

★ ★ ★

We struggled for the rest of the morning to extricate Randolph from the pit and to bury him and Steven beside the trail. I fashioned crosses from saplings, and Norton added a carefully folded sheet of Randolph's sketching paper to each, inscribing their names, and the note, "Died innocently at the hands of craven outlaws. May God have mercy on their souls." I said a tearful prayer for them once we had finished our grim duty.

Each of the bandits had a .31 bullet hole in his forehead. We pushed them into the pit with the horses and rolled stones and brush on top of them and sent their own horses, stripped of their saddles, galloping up the trail after Nast. Norton posted a sign beside the pit that read: "Murderers, killed in an ambush of their own devising, by honest travellers, on this 15 August, 1859. May God find it in His Grace to pardon them."

★ ★ ★

The ride back to Blossom took three days. Three days of lamentation and recriminations as we slowly wound our way down along the Pit, minding every inch of ground that we had to cross. I tried to tell Norton that it was fate that brought us all together on that trail, at that moment in time. A sad, sad fate. And God's will—how else could we account for it?—that we emerged unscathed while our friends had perished. I related the story of Nast, his hateful presence on the *Coventry*, and said he had received his just rewards at Norton's hand. I complimented my friend on having saved us with his crack shooting.

"We wouldn't be here if it weren't for you," I told him.

"Two of us aren't, because of me," he replied.

"Norton," I said, "you can't blame yourself for this."

"Who *should* bear the blame of it, then?"

"Nast and his pals, I'd say."

"Who was it began this adventure?"

"Please, Norton. Next you'll be saying it all started with your being born."

"That's true. I am to blame. I had to tell that silly story and send us all searching for . . . an egg! I couldn't go on without it. And now two of my friends have paid with their lives to help me find it."

"Well, then you must do some good with it," I said.

"I don't have it."

"What do you mean? You didn't give it to those cowards."

"No," he said, "I gave it to Rufus. An investment in his flying ship."

drays and streetcars, indifferent to their presence. He lost weight, forgot to bathe, and was quickly becoming a close cousin to the vagabonds who dozed in the doorways and pissed on the cots at the Jubilee Mission.

So to buoy his spirits, one day, on a lark, I brought Norton some clothes from Henninger's haberdashery—the ones hanging from the nails in the back room that had been traded in years ago by their owners for new, less conspicuous outfits. For a few dollars, I bought an officer's formal coat, dark navy serge with plenty of golden braids, and gray trousers with red satin stripes down the leg. Abe Warner contributed the saber, the carved serpent walking stick from Java, the Kossuth hat with the white cockade.

"Have Norton come see me," Abe said as I was leaving. "It's not right that he stays to himself like this."

"Norton thinks he let you down too, Abe, after what you invested in him."

"Oh, nonsense," Abe replied, but he could not conceal how badly he felt about the whole affair. "Nobody blames him. This city is full of beached hopes, and enough water to float them again. He just needs for the tide to turn and he'll be sailing like crackers."

"Awwk Grandfather," Pedro added, removing his beak from Abe's drink. "Mind the mundungus."

I brought the costume back to Norton's room, where he sat on the bed, gazing out the window at the foggy

September evening. A mist had drifted in off the ocean and chilled the air.

"Try this on," I nudged him. "You'll feel like a new man."

This was, perhaps, not such an idle expression in those days, since many had changed not only their coats and hats in San Francisco, but their names and the characters that they presented to the world as well. You could never tell who exactly might be sitting next to you on the streetcar—a millionaire who appeared to be a mechanic; a lady of the evening dressed in the finest lace and silks; a prominent lawyer, fresh from the Hamman Baths on Grant Street, in the caftan and fez of a Turk; an unassuming small man with a pointed head who was, if you could but ascertain the truth about him, the champion rifle marksman of the country and capable of bending crowbars with his bare hands. Appearances are that slippery.

There was the famous case of Talbot Green, who rose to prominence in the city. He even had Green Street named after himself and was planning to run for mayor when Cynthia Courtney saw him close up at the cotillion and recognized him as Paul Geddes, who had robbed a bank in Philadephia and come out West with the proceeds. Talbot packed his shirts and vanished into the night. People laughed and said he had probably changed his stripes again and was sure to be a governor somewhere by now.

To my surprise, Norton dutifully changed into his unfamiliar trousers and allowed me to hold the officer's coat open while he slid into it. I set the hat on his head, and he inspected what he could of the outfit in the small mirror above his dresser.

"Let's walk outside and have a proper look in one of the shop windows," I suggested. "It's nearly dark. No one will recognize you. They'll think you're a visiting commodore."

On the street he could see himself reflected fully in the windows, and I thought I detected a slight smile of approval. "This is how an emperor should look," I ventured.

"Indeed it is," he replied, and then, in frustration, he cried out, "Oh, what's the use. I'm ruined. I'm not fit to be anything. "

"Norton, all will change. You'll see." I attempted to quiet his anguish. "You'll have a new business going again soon."

"I can't go into business again. I don't have the strength for it, or the inclination. I'm not fit for anything but oblivion, and if you hadn't taken my pistols I might have found it."

"Listen, Norton. Why don't we walk over to Abe's and have a drink. Pedro is no doubt cursing in Russian by now."

"I'm not in the mood for levity."

"Then we can simply walk along and you can enjoy being Emperor of San Francisco this evening."

"Yes, and tomorrow what will I be?" he replied sullenly.

"Well then, tomorrow you can decide."

"What do you mean?"

"Just that. Decide tomorrow if you wish to remain the Emperor."

"But how could I? What would people say?"

"What do you care? You're ruined anyway. You've nothing to lose. Besides, there are plenty of people playing at being many things on the streets of this city. Many of them are considered illustrious citizens, and we all know they're playing a part. 'All the world's a stage,' my dear Norton. You know that."

"But the idea is insane."

"Why is it insane? You have always told me that you thought you were descended from royal parentage. Why don't you just seize your patrimony?"

"But I'll not be a madman like that Coombs who calls himself George Washington the Second, or that demented wretch who strips to his underwear and carries on about pain. I can't become one of those."

"Of course not, " I agreed. "No standing about and shouting or carrying placards, no begging and cajoling, no pathetic shuffling, no posing. Your office must be dignified, your empire beyond reproach. It must reach for the highest principles."

"And what if I don't succeed?"

"If you don't succeed, Norton, I'll give you back your pistols."

XXVI

I never did have to return Norton's revolvers to him. Circumstances intervened the following day at the Post Office when one of the clerks I knew inquired after Norton: Didn't I know him, was he still around, he'd stopped collecting his mail. Could I tell him that there were letters for him, and they'd be pitched in a week with the rest of the dead ones if he didn't call for them?

The next evening Norton burst into my room with the letters. Several were from creditors who claimed that he still owed them money and threatened certain actions if payment was delayed much longer. He laughed at these, ruefully, and cast them aside. But there was another, on plush stationary, that he pushed across the table for me to read.

It was from a solicitor in England whom Norton had, during his first years in the city, commissioned to establish his true paternity. He had given the attorney several thousands of dollars to secure the proof that would confirm his title. The funds had been exhausted, the solicitor wrote, but he was "on the brink of discovery. Comte de ———, a confidant of Charles X, has confided in me that you were the happy issue of a liaison between the old king, while he was in exile, and a noble Englishwoman of the highest rank, whose name may not be divulged because of what would surely be the ensuing scandal. The identity of this confidant must also remain secret at his insistence until it is within my power to transfer to him the necessary monetary assurances, at which point, he swears on his honor, he will produce the most extraordinary and incontrovertible documents to support this worthy cause. If you would most kindly remit the sum of £5,000 sterling, or that amount in American dollars through a letter of transfer from your bank, I believe that we may quickly see this affair through to its exceedingly happy conclusion for all parties concerned. I will await your word and always remain your humble servant..."

"You see," Norton said. "Now do you still believe that it was all my mother's fabrication?"

"But Norton, this may all be a ruse," I countered.

"How can you, of all people on this earth," he asked, "speak to me of ruses?"

★ ★ ★

Norton was a changed man. He appeared at my door the next evening in his regalia and insisted that we walk to Abe's together. He carried himself proudly on the street, despite the gawking and the guffaws as we went by, greeted an open-mouthed Abe with nonchalant affability, and requested the use of Abe's private table in the back.

"I have decided what it is I need to do, and I would like you to help me," Norton said once we were seated with our toddies.

Behind us an alter of scrimshawed tusks and the bicuspids of baleens rose up into the smoky dark among the cobwebs that hung like icicles from the ceiling.

"I wish to declare myself."

"What do you mean?" I replied.

"I need to compose a statement—to make it official."

"What kind of statement?"

"Well, what does an Emperor do when he wants to announce something?"

"He proclaims."

"Then that is what I wish to do."

Abe supplied us with paper, and I took his dictation. We haggled over the wording and the governing powers of an emperor and what such a monarch should say and what he might do first, seeing as he was taking over another country. We went through half a dozen attempts. But here is what finally emerged:

At the preemptory request of a large majority of these citizens of these United States, I, Joshua Norton, formerly of Algoa Bay, Cape of Good Hope, and now for the past nine years and ten months of San Francisco, California, declare and proclaim myself Emperor of these U.S., and in virtue of the authority thereby in me vested, do herby order and direct the representatives of the different States of the Union to assemble in the Musical Hall of this city on the 1st day of February next, then and there to make such alterations in the existing laws of the Union as may ameliorate the evils under which the country is laboring, and thereby cause confidence to exist, both at home and abroad, in our stability and integrity.

"Now, how do I get the citizenry to read it?" he asked.

"You might try to publish it somewhere," I offered.

"Good," he rejoined. "How about the *Bulletin*?"

"Norton, I don't know. I could sound Fitch out about it, but..."

"No, that won't be necessary. I'll bring it to him myself."

Before we left, Norton made a fresh copy of his famous edict in his own hand and signed it, with a flourish: "Norton I, Emperor of the United States." He included Mexico under his protection awhile later.

The next day, while I was downstairs on the presses, in marched Norton, right up to George Fitch, and set the paper on the edge of his desk. Fitch barely looked up, and by the time Norton's surprising appearance registered upon him, the Emperor had turned and left the *Bulletin*'s offices. When I had returned, Fitch came over to my desk and waved the proclamation in front of me.

"You know this Norton, don't you?" Without waiting for my reply, he pressed on. "Is he as addled as all this?"

"Well, I don't know about that. But he has been through a great ordeal and has lost everything."

Fitch had a good nose for a story and was hungry for any edge he could get on the competition.

"Then we'll print it for the pure drama of it. Lear on the heath, and all that. 'Blow ye hurricanoes, blow!'"

XXVII

So Norton donned his royal uniform, proclaimed, and a legend was born.

The first months were not easy. He was stopped in the streets and asked if he was going to a costume ball, or readying himself to join the naval corps, or seeking employment as a doorman at one of the posh new hotels that had sprung up around town. And then there were the outright jeers, the taunts and the ridicule that came to the lips of some as he approached them. They would vacate the sidewalk and extravagantly bow themselves into the street or a shop doorway.

"Oh, excuse me . . . Your Highness. Is that what we are now to call you? Or is it your Empireness? I am sorry to be cluttering the pavement with my miserable presence when majesty wishes to stroll down the street!"

★ ★ ★

But Norton was not to be deterred. A new energy and resolve now filled his days. He wrote the solicitor in England at once and demanded that the gentleman Comte de ——— tell the world the truth, and then, once revenues began to accrue, the reward that he requested would be forthcoming. He signed the letter "Norton I."

The businessman in him also came to his assistance at this time, and gave him the idea of raising the revenue for his legal expenses by offering bonds of twenty-five and later fifty cents as investments in his empire. He called the bonds his taxes, something his honorable subjects should be happy to pay to live under his reign. He visited me at Mrs. Palmer's, where I had returned to live, while he stayed on in his room on Stockton, even though she had offered him a special rate. He thanked her for her kindness but insisted that he could not continue to rely forever on the benevolence of others. He would have to make his own way. To this end, the bonds. He asked me to print the certificates for him in red and green ink, the favored colors of his empire, with a picture, to add a feminine touch, that Randolph had once drawn of Nellie Cole, the belle of the Bella Union, who adored Norton and always had a smile for him and kind words and a few dollars that she would slip into his pocket.

It was then that I must allow that I had some concerns for his state of mind. I worried that Norton might find himself in trouble with the city authorities, but he maintained that such transactions were entirely legal. Though not entirely convinced, because I had encouraged him earlier, I now went ahead and did as he requested. After all, I reasoned, people could see what they were buying, there was no intention to deceive, and the sums were insignificant. It seemed like a harmless thing. And many bought these bonds, which he sold in the streets, in restaurants and saloons, and in front of hotels. With each sale, he personally signed the bond and affixed his seal, the face of the one-franc coin dipped in ink and pressed against the paper, after which he entered the date when the bonds would be redeemable, with interest—1880—by which time, of course, he would have his titles and his fortune in the bank.

He assiduously studied the newspapers again, at the Mechanic's Institute reading room or other places where he was made welcome, and he had opinions on every matter of the day, which he was anxious to express, especially now that he had the public's ear, bemused or otherwise. For his part, Fitch was only too happy to help bend that ear. He published Norton's decrees in the *Bulletin*, and soon everyone joined the spectacle, sniggering about the Emperor in their columns, or rallying to his defense, as some did on the occasion when a green constable threw Norton into jail on the charge of vagrancy for wandering into the Palace Hotel to avail himself of the newspapers and to rest his limbs, something that the management had permitted him to do for years. And it was not long before other papers also began publishing Imperial edicts that were penned by one of the numerous pretenders to the Emperor's throne.

Norton's daily activities were watched with great interest. It was duly noted where he might be seen, what theatrical performances and lectures he attended, the establishments he graced with his presence, and the affairs of state he may have conducted there. Eddie Jump, who wasn't fit to sharpen Randolph's pencils, drew pictures of Norton with those two alley dogs, Lazarus and Bummer, all three of them stuffing their cheeks at the free lunch counter at Martin & Horton's. That much of it was true. Norton took his midday meal where it was offered gratis to him, as it was throughout the city to anyone who had the five cents for a glass of beer. And the picture made the trio famous. But Norton despised those mutts. They were always about his legs, which were unsteady and swollen from poor circulation, and it made him furious to be lampooned like that. He very nearly put a cobblestone through the window of a bookshop on Powell that hung a copy of the cartoon in its window, and then had the temerity to advertise that it was Bookseller to the Emperor.

Norton took his duties seriously, and these responsibilities only grew with the years. He issued a proclamation calling for peace at the beginning of the Civil War; he demanded the abolition of slavery and a corrupt California legislature; he castigated Congress and city officials alike. He put the engineering skill that few knew he had to work when he invented a railroad switch that greatly reduced the number of accidents that occurred and saved many lives on the line that had now reached the Bay from the East Coast. He inspected the new cable cars and pronounced them sound. He was present, in a new pair of gold-braided epaulets, when General Grant visited the city. And Norton dreamed grand dreams: a bridge should be built, he ordered in one of his proclamations, across the Bay from Oakland to San Francisco, bringing the terminus of the railroad into the city. You can guess the uproar that idea started, and there were some who said that he finally had lost whatever slim wits he still managed to possess.

Through sun and showers, chill and mist, as time passed his days took on a regular rhythm, like the steady beating of a well-oiled turbine, from his morning papers in the reading room of the Empire House Hotel, next door to his new lodgings on Commercial Street, to Portsmouth Square, where Marcelin, the flower seller, with great ceremony, pinned a flower on the Emperor's lapel and where he held court in good weather with the other senior counselors who had seats on the public benches. Ah How, his Chinese chamberlain, sat beside him, nodding his agreement with the Emperor's every statement, chasing away a peevish boy or gawking sightseer when either action was required. Perhaps a bite to eat at one of the saloons, and then an afternoon tour of inspection in some quarter of the city, to check the progress of one of Teddy Hightalling's building crews constructing Charlotte Palmer's new hotel, or to visit Abe's menagerie and the little monkey who loved to sit on Norton's shoulders.

He appeared at a different church or synagogue each sabbath, so that he would not appear to be favoring any one sect or religion, and he advocated the creation of one sabbath for Christians and Jews alike so that the Jewish population of the city would not be penalized by the laws that closed shops on Sundays.

People tipped their hats to him as he passed by in his swallow-tailed jacket and his plumed hat, steadily tapping his way with his walking stick, his left hand proudly resting on the hilt of his saber. It was quite a sight he cut, even in the rain, with his lacquered Chinese umbrella held aloft, strolling past the gardens of the homes in Rincon Point, staring out to sea at Cliff House, nodding to the families ambling along the paths that wound through Woodward's Gardens.

It was in Woodward's that he met the late love of his life, Addie Ballou, as she sketched on one of the secluded benches in a shaded by-way of the garden. He stopped to admire her work, and they fell into earnest conversation. She had led a life of some renown; a nurse with the 32nd Wisconsin during the Civil War, she ministered to the regiment through battles and disease and earned its undying gratitude. After those trying years, she began a career as an orator, speaking out for women's suffrage and other causes, and while she was thus involved she cultivated her growing interests in painting and poetry.

She abhorred violence, she told Norton that day among the eucalyptus, the pepper trees, and the agapanthus.

So did he, and it would never be tolerated in his Empire.

She opposed capital punishment.

So did he, and regarded execution as a barbaric and unholy practice.

She claimed suffrage for all citizens.

It was one of the cornerstones of his political thought.

She lamented the unsanitary conditions that still plagued the city and led to virulent fevers.

He concurred and promised to work for a sanitary rejuvenation of the Bay.

★ ★ ★

Soon Addie and Norton were seen strolling together everywhere about the city—in Woodward's, at Seal Rocks, along Powell where the new mansions for Leland Stanford and Mark Hopkins were competing for the best view of the Bay, or across the Bay in Berkeley to the School for the Deaf and Blind. Each month Addie went to visit the afflicted there. Norton accompanied her on these excursions and stopped with her to lean against the long, simple fence in front of the school to survey this beautiful valley. He would hold his umbrella above her, to shield her from the sun while she composed a watercolor of the scene.

She dropped a glove, he gallantly retrieved it.

She volunteered for work at a hospital for the indigent on the waterfront, he escorted her.

When she wished to try her hand at riding one of the new velocipedes that were careening down the hills of the city, he selected an even lane for her to learn to maintain her balance, and then a gentle hill where she might practice her declinations. He held the machine steady while she mounted it, he helped her up when she spilled into the rhododendrons at the bottom of the hill.

She insisted that he call her, familiarly, "Addie," and she, in turn, named him her "Dear Emp."

She painted his portrait.

He flamboyantly gave her a check for two hundred fifty dollars, which he did not have, but which was honored by the bank nonetheless and kept as a souvenir.

She even visited his humble room on Commercial Street. He begged her not to think ill of him because of its shabby appearance.

"If you only knew the things that I have seen, Dear Emp," she told him, "you would not need to make such a request of me."

He did not tell me what happened there—he was, of course, a gentleman.

But his neighbor Frankie Frisch reported to me later that there was laughter in the Emperor's room till very late at night whenever Addie Ballou came to visit, and quiet whisperings.

★ ★ ★

And then, as suddenly as she appeared in Norton's life, she was gone—to Oregon to sue for the life of a luckless lad condemned to hang, then to Chicago and New York in the interests of winning women's suffrage, to Ohio to visit family, to Australia to paint for several years at the invitation of a wealthy patron.

Norton knew he could not expect her to stay with him, a free spirit like Addie, he told me later. It was understood between them from the start. But the head may promise one thing, while the heart confides another.

XXVIII

After Addie left, it was as though the light in the Emperor began to dim. He grew taciturn and melancholy, and let everything go again—his clothes, his grooming, his eating habits, his whole person. Although he forced himself to continue his daily inspections of the city, they became desultory, dejected, and dangerous, for he was distracted when he should have been alert, as though he sought an encounter with a tram or trap, and the end to his suffering which that might bring.

For its part, the city continued to show him off in its puffed up, bleary way once the railroad had breached the continent and people were enticed to come West to see the sights: the Yosemite and China Town, the sea lions at the cliffs, and the Emperor, roughly in that order. Some enterprising souls had even cashed in on little china statues of Norton, which you could take back with you to Cleveland or Providence, along with the stereoptican pictures that Muybridge, the famous photographer, took of him, posed on a velocipede, furiously peddling—or so it seemed, until you looked closely at the picture and saw that the contraption was leaning against a fence and its rider was exhausted.

★ ★ ★

It had been Muybridge's idea to take the picture as a way of raising funds for Norton's well-being, a small repayment for a debt of honor that he owed to Norton, he believed. Although the two men's lives were vastly divergent, it seems that they crossed in the person of Harry Larkyns, a profligate and cheat who gave himself the title of Major and then under the cover of respectability insinuated himself into the lives of decent, unsuspecting folks.

Larkyns, who sometimes supported himself as a reporter when he could not dupe others into providing him with his income, had lost his job on the *Post* because of his utter indolence. His replacement was a meek, inoffensive man named Coppinger, whom Larkyns blamed for his dismissal and therefore sought to make his life a misery. Whenever Coppinger found himself in an establishment with Larkyns, the Major would immediately subdue the smaller man and, prying open Coppinger's mouth, spit into his throat. This had earned the victim the name Cuspidor Coppinger and the gleeful scorn of the brave drinking men who kept company with Larkyns or wished to avoid a conflict with him.

One day Coppinger happened to be standing at the bar of Martin and Horton's with the Emperor, when in swung an already tipsy Larkyns.

"Ah, well, if it isn't the Cuspidor!" Larkyns cried out above the noise of the crowd, biting off the tip of his cigar and chewing it into a pulp. He made his way for Coppinger, who cowered next to Norton.

Larkyns reached Coppinger, seized him by the nose and, twisting it, forced Coppinger to his knees. Larkyns was commencing to wrench open his victim's mouth when he felt the point of something at his own throat.

"Leave him be, sir," the Emperor said quietly.

Larkyns looked at Norton in astonishment and immediately released Coppinger.

"Leave him be," the Emperor repeated. "Do not touch this man again, sir, or I vow I will cut you down."

A speechless Larkyns backed away from Norton's blade and out the door. He hurled curses from the threshold back at Norton, but from that day on, he did leave Coppinger alone.

Had the Emperor been forced to keep his own promise to the Major, the city would have been relieved of Larkyns much sooner. As it happened, fate left that task to Muybridge.

Harry Larkyns had ingratiated himself into Muybridge's family and later seduced Muybridge's young wife, Flora, while her white-haired husband was away. And Muybridge was frequently away on photographic expeditions—in the Yosemite, in the north during the Modok War, in the Wasatch, in Utah. Major

Larkyns took up his post in Muybridge's bed and arrogantly sent his shirts out to be laundered with his host's. He had succeeded in getting Flora with his child when the affair was discovered, and Muybride secretly sent his wife away to Oregon to raise the infant, forbidding her to communicate with Larkyns. But the Major discovered where she was through the midwife who had delivered the child and had remained a go-between for Flora and Larkyns. Then, regretting her complicity, the midwife told Muybridge about the letters she had received from the two lovers, and Muybridge did the only thing a gentleman could. He tracked Larkyns to where he was staying near Calistoga, before leaving for Oregon to rendezvous with Flora, and he shot Larkyns dead. The jury refused to convict Muybridge. They would have done the same thing themselves, all said afterwards.

I digress to tell you this because I am sometimes asked if I think the Emperor was insane. While I must grant that a life such as the one Norton lived those last twenty years must seem to be anything but the operation of a sound mind, was his defense of Coppinger the action of a madman, as many have claimed him to be?

Most people were content to see the Emperor from a distance, not close enough to smell the sweat on his clothes because he could not afford to send his things out for proper cleaning, or to buy fresh new ones. They did not want to know about the lamentable condition of his feet from walking miles and miles every day because he could not stand the four walls of his small room, even though those ragged quarters contained communications from our nation's leaders and the crowned heads of Europe, several even expressing their sympathy with his plight and their hope that he would soon take his rightful place among them. I have inspected the telegrams, read the letters, from Lincoln and Queen Victoria and the Tsar of Russia, and would gladly repeat their contents to any who might wish some further testimony to the curious and persisting truth of Norton's claim.

Although folks may have dismissed Norton's presence with a scornful laugh, they did keep the bonds that he issued, the proceeds from which barely covered his lodgings and food. Some people maintained that he made a tidy profit from the tourists when he met the trains from the East in Oakland with a pocketful of scrip, or that the bonds would someday be of value—who could know about these things? In the end there were no fortunes to be made from his empire. And Norton knew this too, like he knew the other demarcations of his celebrity. While a saloon keeper would give you a free meal at the bar where anybody else could get one, the maître d' of the finer restaurants did not want you to appear in his foyer, nor did the theaters always reserve a box seat for you on opening night, no matter how many newspapers reported that as fact.

Some will tell you how the Emperor behaved at church, how he smiled through the sermons and sang all the hymns and even found a few coins for the collection plate, and patted the children's heads at Sunday School like a slightly daffy grandfather.

But this same grandfather was present when the Razor Man, who occupied the corner of Pine and Kearny, worked a treadle to animate his grindstone, as well as several hideous wooden figures, to the accompaniment of his diatribes against the Chinese. Claiming the Chinese brought disease and barbarity to this Christian shore, with his fiendish calls to "get your razor ground," he nearly incited a mob to lynch some poor Chinese nearby for the moral sport of it.

He was only prevented from precipitating such bloodshed by my gentle friend the Emperor, who returned the crowd to their own homes rather than to an assault against innocent Chinese by the simple act of reciting the Lord's Prayer, loudly and passionately, until it silenced the crowd and its provoker.

Was this the act of an insane man? As I have said, in the end our characters—Norton's, mine, or yours—are and will remain unfathomable perplexities.

XXIX

In January of 1880, the year that his bonds fell due for redemption, I was coming down one side of California Street, trying to keep my footing on the steep sidewalk on this rainy evening, January 8th, while Norton was slowly climbing up the other. I recognized his red umbrella. I had not seen him in some time and was eager to catch his attention.

"Norton," I hallooed him. "Emperor!"

He stopped and peered across the street, trying to make out who had called to him. He recognized me, smiled, and tipped his hat in the courtly way he perfected with the years. I saw his mouth move and knew he had sent words across the busy street, and when he saw that I had not comprehended them, he cupped his hand and spoke the words again. Then, without warning, he fell.

I splashed across the street and, with another's help,

raised Norton from the puddle into which he had fallen, propped him against a storefront, and unloosed his top collar button so that he might breathe. But my friend was already gone.

Norton had the largest funeral that had ever been held in the city. Ed Kerrigan, one of the constables at the march, thought more than ten thousand came out in the pouring rain to follow his cortege from the morgue on O'Farrell Street to the Masonic Cemetery, there to see him laid to his final rest. There speeches and many tears were shed as his polished mahogany coffin, covered with flowers, descended into the wet earth. And Georgie Chismore recited his poem in honor of the Emperor:

> *No more through the crowded streets he goes,*
> *With his shambling gait and shabby clothes,*
> *And his furtive glance and whiskered nose—*
> *Immersed in cares of state.*
> *The serpent twisted upon his staff*
> *Is not less careless of idle chaff,*
> *The mocking speech or the scornful laugh,*
> *Than he who bore it late.*

But of course you know it well. And now you see the holes in it.

People want the poetry but not the grand madness that beats in all true poetry. They want the visions—like that bridge soaring over the harbor that Norton even drew for the papers—but not the mad sorrow that creeps in late at night when bridges collapse into that pit along the river, or your beloved vanishes into the mist that shrouds the Golden Gate.

XXX

And me? I stayed out West and kept on at the *Bulletin*, and then at the *Call*, after that was started by a bunch of stray printers like myself, and I even prospered, in my own way, joined the Bohemians and was betrothed to Mrs. Palmer's niece Emily from Connecticut, who came out to visit her aunt and stayed on to marry me. I sang songs to our babies and now to our grandchildren and told them about Chicken Little and David and Goliath, the tale of the Ford brothers and of Job. Emily says these stories are too deep for the little ones, but I say they need to know about the deep, they'll get plenty of the shallow without asking soon enough.

Eventually, my brother, Benjamin, got used up by the mill work in Hartford and came west, too. He didn't like the city, so I took him to visit Eric one spring when they were starting to sow barley and he never came back. He hired on to work for Eric, and then the next year found a place of his own nearby. Nikolai introduced Ben to one of his Russian cousins and now she keeps his house plump with pillows and dumplings and happiness.

Twice a week the earth moves beneath the city, and no one knows if it will swallow us up this time. Preachers in the square say it is the end. They are right, of course; each day could be our last. No doubt this is why I redouble my pace as I pass by, in haste to leave doom behind and be home with those I love. And sometimes when the day is drizzly and old fears have drawn close by, I go to visit Abe, and he and I watch the spiders spinning their webs, doing the fragile, steady work of their lives.